CW01429966

Whispering Campaigns
and other stories

LES BROOKES, author of *Gay Male Fiction Since Stonewall*, writes —

This amazingly diverse collection of stories is sometimes fantastic and dreamlike, sometimes surreal and nightmarish, often playful and satirical, and always transgressive. Some of the stories read like fables, others like cautionary tales. All are unpredictable, and tend, however mildly they begin, to veer off in surprising and sometimes shocking directions. All are laced with wit and black humour. There's a monologue here written for performance, and other pieces, including a dialogue, that cry out for it.

There are strong connections, too. A theme of haunting and guilt links 'Woof', 'Comrades' and 'Last Throw', while 'Same Again, Please', 'Vicarious' and 'Summon Up' focus on frustrated desire and suggestions of unrequited love. Other stories, 'Parenting', 'Family Matters', 'Tidings', take a hard swipe at the follies of education, a theme that also underpins 'Reverses in Time', the opening chapter of a forthcoming novel that ends the collection. The title story is rare in being strictly realist and relates, with subtle innuendo, the dilemma of a gay man mugged by queer-bashers.

One of my favourite stories is 'O My Good Godness', in which a prurient art historian gets a bit more than he bargained for. This story has more than a touch of giggling Firbankian naughtiness, as well as a clear nod to Forster's posthumously published stories in *The Life to Come*. 'Nil Nihil' is a savage Swiftian satire on competitive sport, and perhaps, by extension, the warring, murderous, raping human race. It's not for the faint-hearted and picks up on the theme of games-aversion that runs through the whole collection. All in all, then, a crisp, thoroughly entertaining bundle.

VG LEE, writer and comedian, author of *The Comedienne*; *Always you, Edina*; *Mr Oliver's Object of Desire*, writes —

The author Raymond Carver wrote, 'a writer who has some special way of looking at things and who gives artist expression to that way of looking – that writer may be around for some time'. This very much applies to John Dixon's often intriguing collection of short stories. The majority are written in the first person and the author's voice shone through – for me, the voice worked brilliantly. As I began to relax into the individual stories, it felt as if I'd been admitted into the writer's mind: a highly observant writer with a unique take on life.

Nothing about Dixon's work could be called light or superficial. He cuts deep. Expect the unexpected! Each character's tale is very different: some told with humour, others with regret or disquiet. Two of my personal favourites were the title story, 'Whispering Campaigns', written in the third person, and 'Comrades'.

From the outset of 'Comrades', the reader is made aware that the main character is at odds with their understanding of reality. 'I couldn't leave. I couldn't leave her. I was accountable, as never before, to a fellow human being. She had almost made an offering of herself, a gesture no-one could refuse.'

In both stories, the central characters are outsiders, ill at ease and struggling with an often-hostile world. They are written in vivid detail that never flags. These are absorbing, fascinating accounts and both pack a punch.

By the time I finished reading the collection, I was satisfied: as if I'd eaten a delicious and nourishing meal. Some of the stories offered surprises at their close, nearly all resonated with me. A diverse and compelling collection!

TIM BLACKWELL, author of *The Bingo Caller & other stories*, writes —

Whispering Campaigns offers an impressive breadth of narrative styles; these tales are humorous, macabre, satirical, violent, and often delightfully bizarre. This is not a book for the faint-hearted. Many of these stories are genuinely subversive. They have the courage not to pull punches when taking a swing at sex, art, family values and religion.

All actors will tell you when they pick up a new script, that it is instantly apparent if the lines are well-observed and crafted, making them easy to learn and enjoyable to deliver. This was undoubtedly the case with 'Binkie and the Snowbirds' – which I had the pleasure of performing at The Space Theatre in 2018. Like other stories in this excellent collection of short fiction, 'Binkie and the Snowbirds' entertains with considerable humour and pathos, but never loses sight of the human heart of the story or the substantial themes it deals with – in this case, the lengths a character goes to in an attempt to protect himself from loss.

Skilful prose and speech unite this collection, as does a gay sensibility. Gay characters, so often made invisible in literature, are given voices here. As the title story 'Whispering Campaigns' reminds us, even in today's world, we are constantly in social contexts where there is pressure to keep our sexuality as a love that still doesn't quite dare speak its name. Through these stories, John Dixon does dare to speak, loud and clear.

PETER SCOTT-PRESLAND, writer and performer, author of *The Gay Century* and *Amiable Warriors, a history of the Campaign for Homosexual Equality*, writes —

John Dixon's glittering collection of bonbons offers tales for all tastes, some funny, some creepy, some tragic. And some downright filthy. He does so in elegant, detached prose which reminds the reader of EF Benson or Saki. This could be bland, but – 'He sank into my liquefying innards'? Always there is an arresting phrase to pull you up short.

This works particularly well in the stories which can only be described as dead-pan surrealism of a particularly English kind: the dog-themed 'Woof' and 'Binkie and the Snowbirds', or excursions into the afterlife such as 'Fly-

Trap'. It's an approach that pays dividends too in comedies that flirt with dangerous subjects such as sex within the family.

Dixon is both obsessed and amused by sex. Middle-aged inadequate men falling for at best the unobtainable Adonis, at worst the attractive young thug. He certainly makes sure we are amused as well.

The title story is about a 'queer-bashing' and its psychological aftermath in the workplace. It's acute, and skewers a particular kind of busybody, as the mugging effectively continues in a different form, until ... The story, like several others, is open-ended. Readers are left to their own conclusions. Which is no bad thing at all.

Whispering Campaigns
and other stories

John Dixon

Paradise Press

First published in Great Britain in 2023 by
Paradise Press, BM Box 5700, London WC1N 3XX
www.paradisepress.org.uk

Copyright © 2023 John Dixon

A CIP catalogue record of this book
is available from the British Library

All rights reserved. No part of this book may be
reproduced by any means, electronic or mechanical,
including photocopy or any information storage and
retrieval system without permission in writing from the
publisher.

The right of John Dixon to be identified as the author
of this work has been asserted in accordance with the
Copyright, Designs and Patents Act 1988.

ISBN 978-1-904585-78-7

10 9 8 7 6 5 4 3 2 1

Printed and bound in the UK by
P2D Books Ltd, Westoning

Thanks to Jeff Doorn and Kathryn Bell for
encouragement and help in the preparation of the book

Design and typesetting by Ross Burgess

Cover design by Russell Wilson

Set in Garamond.

To the memory of my good friend and confidant

John Sunley

1932–2019

Contents

Introduction

THE STORIES IN THIS VOLUME were initially published courtesy of the several outlets of the admirable Gay Authors Workshop.

The Workshop was formed in 1978 as a response to the lack of publishing opportunities for gay writers. Membership was to authors who were gay. Their writing did not have to be about gay themes, though it often was. Monthly meetings were held in the front rooms of members' houses, always on a Sunday. Each reading was followed by constructive criticism. Food was usually provided after the readings, or members brought food to share. I joined the Workshop in 2007, having seen an advert in a freebee gay newspaper. I'm glad I did. I learned much from listening to and evaluating the work of other writers, and from receiving criticism of my own efforts.

There was also the possibility of getting into print. This was via four possible outlets. The first was the quarterly Newsletter, which besides being an information bulletin, also printed articles, stories and poems. The fiction was necessarily quite short, around 2,000 words. This was good. It allowed for work of a more experimental nature, not just the compression of what was to become known as 'flash' fiction, but items which crossed the boundary between fiction and non-fiction, and bizarre topics which could not be maintained for any great length without losing credibility. Short and tall, as it were. It also permitted brief monologues and dialogues.

An in-house magazine, called *Gazebo*, had been set up in 1998, and over its nineteen issues, including a women's edition and a poetry edition, it published a range of articles, reviews, and poems. Again, the stories were necessarily short, below 5,000 words, just enough to sustain unlikely situations, or give a taste of a novel in progress. I was lucky to get many rather scurrilous items accepted by the editors of both the Newsletter and Gazebo, and a selection of these are included in the present volume.

The Workshop also established in 1999 its own publishing outlet, Paradise Press, and several titles were published, some by individual authors, some anthologies of short stories and poetry. Naturally I was eager to take advantage of this 'book-format' facility. Paradise Press was not a vanity publisher, but quite a strict self-publishing co-operative with a requirement that work submitted for publication be in part read out at the monthly meetings; and be read in full, evaluated in detail, approved and edited by at least two long-term and published Workshop members; that nothing racist, sexist, libellous, be included, and that come the book production stage the greatest care be taken as to the proof-reading, layout and cover. This is a level of editorial scrutiny that many 'commercial' publishers never had, or no longer have.

It was not always straightforward and never automatic

having one's work accepted. I offered a story, 'Mandorla', to a proposed anthology. It was rejected by the editors on the grounds that though amusing it was felt to be more appropriate for a glossy magazine. I could not quite see this myself, and several years later resubmitted it to another anthology, with a different editor. This time the story was accepted in principle, but I was told said that as there were not enough women contributors to the anthology priority must be given to any forthcoming suitable submissions from women. None were forthcoming. I therefore offered to change my name from John Dixon to Joanna Richardson, and on that basis the story eventually saw the light of day.

The fourth outlet offered by Gay Authors Workshop was publication of a single-author volume. I rather presumptuously enquired if a collection of my short stories, all written well before I joined the group, and only one of which was gay-themed, could be considered for publication. I was informed this was possible, and accordingly every story was read, scrutinised, commented on and 'fine-tuned', including one that had won a prize at the Bridport Short Story Competition, judged by Margaret Drabble. Eventually the collection was accepted for publication by Paradise Press and the page layout, proof reading, book production and cover design kindly done by experienced members of the group. I did not realise at that time how much labour was involved in producing a book.

This was to change. I attended and contributed to most meetings, hosted some and often took the minutes. I also took part in the promotional activities, giving readings in bookshops and libraries. More importantly, I undertook some editorial work, sometimes alone but mostly with a joint editor. Editing is a long-term commitment, demanding, fiddly and eye-tiring. There is a set of house-style rules to give guidance to the physical aspect of the book, but the choice of items to include, the wording of rejection slips, the possible changes needed to ensure inclusion, require understanding and tact.

All the stories in this collection are the product of my time with Gay Authors Workshop, though some stories have appeared elsewhere. 'Comrades' won a short story prize from Chorley Writers (2013) and was initially published by them. The monologue 'Binkie and the Snowbirds' was performed at the Space Theatre's OneFest 2018, by GAW member Tim Blackwell. 'Reverses in Time' is part of the first chapter of a novel, a subsequent chapter of which has appeared online from New London Writers.

John Dixon

January 2023

About the Author

JOHN DIXON has published a collection of short stories *The Carrier Bag*, which includes the Bridport Prize-winning title story, of which Margaret Drabble said 'A tale for our time. A fine use of dialogue from a writer who has his ear to the ground.' He also won a prize from the Chorley Short Story Competition. Other stories appear in the anthologies *People Your Mother Warned You About*, *The*

Best of Gazebo, Eros at Large, and *A Boxful of Ideas.* His novel *Push harder, Mummy, I want to Come Out* is due for publication shortly.

His poems have appeared in *Envoi, Iota, Orbis, Nomad, Chroma, Haiku Quarterly* and in the anthologies *Oysters and Pearls, Coming Clean* and *A Boxful of Ideas.* He has published one collection of poems, *Seeking, Finding, Losing* and is working on another.

He has edited *Poems 2007–2012* by Ivor Treby, co-edited the lyrics and stories of the late Michael Harth, and the anthologies *Coming Clean* and *A Boxful of Ideas.* He edited *Fiction in Libraries* for the Library Association, and co-edited a volume of his father's short stories and his mother's autobiography. Articles on the novelist Brigid Brophy have appeared in the *Shavian* and in the University of Edinburgh symposium, *In Transit.*

Woof

I WAS ABOUT TO INSERT THE KEY in the front door lock when I heard a noise further down the corridor. No way was I going to open the door and give some lurker the opportunity to jump me, and get inside the flat. I'd rather be attacked in the corridor. I moved along and stopped outside someone else's door.

The noise resolved itself into a series of clicks, like a door being unlocked from the inside. And a man came out the flat next to mine. I'd never seen him before. He had a set of keys and I could only assume he was a new neighbour. He nodded, smiled and carefully double-locked.

'How's your dog?' he asked.

I didn't reply. Just nodded. I haven't got a dog.

'Need one round here, don't you?' he said giving a knowing look.

He must know we're not allowed to keep them. Who's he kidding? Most people would have said 'Good morning. How are you?' Not tried to use animals as ice-breakers. I wasn't going to entertain his pleasantries. I smiled back to humour him. Poor man's obviously delusory.

The next day the same thing happened, only in reverse. I

was coming out my flat and the neighbour on the other side was fiddling with the keys to go into hers. She smiled.

'Dog alright? Only hear it at night.'

I forced a smile and nodded. And shrugged when she'd gone.

Neighbours! They come and go. I hear them more than I see them. The walls of the flats are thin. You can hear drills, hammering, water pipes, thermostats, light switches, spin dryers, and, of course, hoovers, especially when they bang on the skirting board. You can predict daily routines, or if a neighbour works nights. Some noises though are oddly muffled. It's hard to distinguish between voices and snoring, a sneeze or a cough. I've never thought of myself as being noisy. I can't imagine why they assume I have a dog.

I did have a dog once. Dunbar he was called. When he was disobedient – which wasn't often – I called him Dumbo. He was better company than any human. He went white round the jaws and eyes. His legs began to fail him. Once he got out his basket he could make his way round the flat OK. But there was no more going down the flights of stairs, no more walkies. And that posed problems for me. I was prepared to put up with them for his sake. The neighbours – the ones at that time – said it would be kinder to have him put down. It was almost their way of saying 'We never told on you for having a dog, but now's your chance to get rid of what you should never have had.' What a fool I was to take notice of them! I shouldn't have listened. Whenever I see someone out with a dog I reproach myself. I'd have another if I could, but the rules have been tightened. You couldn't get away with it now. The neighbours might not tell on you, but one way or another they'd let you know that they knew. Oh, yes.

What their game is now I can't imagine. 'How's your dog?' he'd said, and she'd said 'Only hear it at night.' What were they on about? Was I missing something I should have cottoned on to? Should I listen out just in case?

I tried to keep myself awake that night, but kept nodding off. The same the next night. But then I was woken. Woken by a barking noise. It was like a dog barking in its sleep. Not a full bark, muffled. Like old Dunbar made when he was dreaming of chasing cats or intruders. Sometimes he used to wake himself up. More often he half woke, and his eyelids fluttered and showed the eye-whites. He sometimes bared his teeth. Once I intervened and woke him. 'Hey, what's up?' I said patting him. Instead of greeting me, he snarled. He must have been dreaming of thieves, and thought he was being attacked. He soon came to and realised he was safe. He meant no harm. After that I always let him bark on. None of the previous neighbours complained, though they told me he always howled when I went out and left him alone.

It was distinctly a bark I heard. No getting away from that. The neighbours had heard it. I'd doubted them, but now I've heard it. They were right. The neighbours were right. The neighbours on either side, that is. There weren't any neighbours above. The flat had been empty for months. It was security boarded to prevent squatters living there, and making it a knocking shop or a den for drugs. The flat below was always noisy. The old girl's deaf, and not conscious of all the racket she makes. She certainly hasn't got a dog. She's hardly able to look after herself, let alone a pet.

I nodded off. There it was again. Where was it coming from? And again. Very close. It stopped when I woke. This happened three or four times. Then I realised – and woke to an almost higher degree of consciousness – it was me. I was barking in my sleep.

No, it can't be. Couldn't ever be. I wouldn't ever let it. Not something you admit to. Not to yourself. Let alone outsiders.

My mind panicked. What if it were true? Why should it be? Why? Yes, why? Perhaps I'd been thinking of Dunbar before I went to sleep. I always used to tuck him up in his basket last thing at night, pull the blanket up so just his nose was showing. Had that been it? The last thing on my waking mind had prompted a dream? It happens.

I must make sure not to relive these old routines. I got up. It was in the small hours but I moved round all the furniture so it was nothing like Dunbar would have known. The next night I left the radio on. The night after that I read a salacious book before nodding off. All to no avail. The barking still came to me.

So? Should I pretend I had a dog? Confirm what the neighbours already think? Not deny it? Make a feature of it? A talking point? Let them call in the authorities. They won't find anything.

But how would that help? What if I fell asleep on a bus or a train? Even lying on a park bench? I'd never been told I snore, or talk in my sleep, or talk to myself. Let alone bark!

No, to deal with a problem you have to accept there is one. I half-doubted there was. I needed verification. I couldn't obtain it by myself. I suppose I could leave a tape running when I went to bed, but it might run out before I reached a deep enough sleep. I needed someone there to record the sounds, turn on the tape when the sounds began, turn over the tape, and keep turning the tapes until there was proof positive. Not just their say-so, but enough to convince me. But I knew no-one whom I could confide in to that extent. Not a neighbour. A doctor or a shrink would lock you up.

Oh, forget it. For the time being at least. It's not urgent. It could have been going on for months. Let me be the only person who knows.

The uncertainty nagged. It begged to be checked out. And it could be done. I just had to allow a stranger to watch me sleep. Why not? Dunbar was trusting and vulnerable in his sleep. It was reassuring to hear him bark in his sleep. I knew he was OK even though I couldn't see him breathing under his rug. He was loyal, unquestioning – even after I'd made the decision to have him put down. The vet on the phone didn't even query my request. Meant nothing to him. Two of them came in a van. One came up and helped me take Dunbar down the stairs. He'd always got on with strangers. He thought he was going for a walk. We lifted him into the back of the van.

The vets were very friendly. Dunbar was reassured because I was there. And they were nice to me and I was nice to them. They had a job to do. Perhaps in certain circumstances justified. One of them took out a syringe – and I think Dunbar knew. He didn't struggle. Oh, the look he gave me! It was goodbye and forgiveness. He forgave me. Thanked me even. I stroked his head and he fell asleep.

It all comes back as never before. Better I'd let him live. I could have coped if he'd died here naturally. What if I'd died in the flat, leaving him alone? He'd have barked for help – for my sake, bless him. But I? No, I just humoured him, abused his trust, almost intended it all along.

What difference to the farmer who fattens up the willing, greedy goose? Or leads on the skipping lamb or kid, and nestles it down before the ritual slitting? Or strokes the angora or chinchilla before giving it a rabbit punch? Or throws down corn so the chicken stretches out its neck?

I need to escape such thoughts and settle this matter. Incontrovertibly. On tape. I need someone here while I sleep. To turn the tapes. Not a neighbour, no. Too embarrassing for a friend. A complete stranger.

Asking a woman would be too much of a lead-on. Bound to have consequences. She could use the tape against me. Less come-back likely from a man. Give him a drink, cigarette, snack. Sweetener.

There are people out there who come to life at night.

Places to go. Pubs at closing time, gathering points under bridges round makeshift fires. People who would do anything for a small consideration. Anything legal considered. This wasn't illegal.

I looked in the mirror – a bit white round the sideburns, thin at the top. No matter. I hid all I could. And disguised the rest. In the dark I felt more confident. I had something to offer. I was a patron giving a commission, creating employment, providing free lodging for the night.

I barely looked at him. I didn't want him to see my face. I told the minimum. He agreed. I took him back a circuitous route, avoiding streetlamps. I was glad for once all the lights in the corridor had been vandalised. I'd had the foresight to remove the number from my front door. I'd left the curtains open so we could see without the light on.

He looked round the room and nodded.

'Feel free,' I said. 'Make yourself at home. I want you to …' And I told him. He said nothing and showed no surprise. And I felt I ought to say something more.

'It's like this,' I went on, 'I'm about to begin a relationship – but first need to check out some things. Silly things. If I snore or make any kind of noise whatever. And talk in my sleep. I must know that. It could incriminate me. Be used against me.'

He gave an understanding nod and spoke for the first time, 'Don't wanna give yourself away.'

'That's exactly it. Not even under torture.'

I pulled the duvet right over me and snuggled down. I

must have woken myself up. I couldn't work out where I was. The light was on. It all looked different, as if things had been moved round. I panicked, and thought the man had run off and pocketed all he could. But he was still there. He turned and I saw his face clearly for the first time. He reminded me of one of the vets.

He pointed to a pile of tapes. 'All full. Both sides.' He smiled sadly as if he had all the evidence for a diagnosis. He shook his head, seeming to say 'I'm so sorry. There's nothing else I can do.' He leaned forward, and held out a syringe.

Same Again, Please

'WHY IS IT?' SAID JEROME, 'that the parents of gay people always live such a bloody long time?'

All his friends had elderly parents, so did several neighbours and most of his undeclared work colleagues.

'Is it a universal truth – or just my reading of a situation I'm all too familiar with?'

He threw up his hands in exasperation.

'And as for you, you needn't think you're going to out-live me! You'd love that, wouldn't you? Then you could make out I was a saint and never married because I was … so, so happy to devote my life to looking after you. Well, I haven't had a life – you stole it – and now I'm about to retire. To what? I work hard and forfeit every-thing just to … to … God, the years I've spent clearing up your phlegm and diarrhoea – and spooning out a bland, knifeless diet into your toothless gums. And you're even too deaf to hear what I'm saying. Why don't you just die!'

He finished tucking up his father in bed, then gently put a glass of fresh water on the bedside table.

'And now perhaps …'

Jerome's only escape was at night. He tip-toed out of the house and headed straight for the local park. He walked round and round and when it was obvious there was no new talent worth following he spoke to one of the regulars, several of whom had elderly relatives.

'By the way, I forget to ask – how's your old father?'

'Mother, actually.'

'Sorry.'

'Don't be. There's not much difference at that age. How's your … your one?'

Jerome shrugged. 'Life goes on.'

He walked round the circuit again and continued the conversation when they passed later.

'Where's old Harry these days? Haven't seen him for weeks?

'His father died.'

'Oh, dear.'

'And Harry doesn't come over here anymore.'

There was a long pause. 'He goes over the Flats. He says there's a lot of new talent there.'

'Really? It's so difficult to get back from there in time.'

'Surely it doesn't matter, now you're retired.'

No, thought Jerome, I don't suppose it does.

He found comfort from these nightly quests. He returned home better disposed to his father.

'The poor old man. He must be confused, in pain. No wonder he's so irritable. It won't be for much longer.'

When Daddy approached the age of a hundred Jerome spent hours looking for an appropriate card. There were cards for retirement, bereavement, sixty, seventy and eighty. Any age beyond that was obviously not commercially viable. Jerome was forced into a scissors-and-paste effort.

'Daddy will never notice the joins.'

He handed the card to his father early on the birthday morning along with a present. His father seemed grateful. Several other cards arrived, but Jerome's one was given pride of place, in the centre of the mantelpiece. Later that day an official looking envelope – embossed and crested – was delivered by special mail. It was the traditional congratulations telegram from the Queen. Daddy was well pleased. 'Put it in the middle of the mantelpiece. Move yours. This one's – from the real Queen.'

Jerome said nothing and went ahead with the birthday schedule.

'We're going out for a spin,' and he settled his father into the wheelchair. 'Let's go to the park.'

His father said nothing. Jerome felt in control pushing the chair. He could not see his father's face, just his hands plucking and gathering at the blanket round his knees. Equally Daddy could not see him and Jerome was able to wave to his friends. He pointed to things and shouted. 'Look at the bandstand. They've just finished repainting it.'

His father said nothing. Jerome pointed beyond the grass to the far hedge.

'And look at those lovely rhododendrons over there.'

'Yes,' said Daddy, pointing somewhat nearer, 'and look at those pansies on the grass. Is this where you come when you go out after midnight?'

Jerome let go the handles of the wheelchair.

When Daddy died, and all the funeral and inheritance arrangements were over and all the documentation safely filed away, Jerome decided to move. He found a small townhouse, purpose built, but in an old style, and equidistant between the park and the Flats. He had a house-warming get-together for the regulars from the park.

'My life is going to change,' he announced. 'Bye-bye to Clandestine-by-Night. I'll to go out whenever and wherever I want, and invite round whomsoever I wish! Most of all, I am free to settle down to form a proper relationship.'

Jerome visited the park by day and sat on the bench watching the passers-by. He had missed out on the fun and games of childhood and half wanted to join in the sports that were being played, or at least teach the players the rules of games he had never played himself.

A regular noticed him and said, 'Can see what you're up to. Some young people like older men – especially if they've never had a father figure.'

'Well,' Jerome replied sharply, 'that wouldn't be me then, would it? And I wouldn't want to perpetuate what I suffered from.'

In fact, the footballers did not interest him. He did not care who won, and found it an anti-climax when the victors shook hands with the losers. He appreciated their muddy legs, the sweaty shirts and shorts and the dishevelled hair, but he much preferred a broken nose, a black eye, missing teeth, bruises, tattoos and scars – someone to take back and offer sanctuary from the police or rival gangs.

One youth who fitted the description stayed overnight, came back a second time and moved in. He only had a few belongings.

'I travel light,' Vince said, 'and if I get anything I sell it quick.'

Soon all Jerome's time and space were disrupted. Vince invited round his friends, some rougher than even Jerome would have dared to smile at. And then, just as quickly, they all disappeared, Vince included.

Two days later a policeman knocked at the front door. He apologised and said, 'Look, I think there's been some mistake, but I've got to check it out. Your address has been given as the residence of a gentleman – who claims that the owner of the residence will know him by the name of – Vince.'

'That's no mistake. But he's not here at the moment. Do you know where is he? He's got nowhere else to go but here.'

'I see. You do know him then. He's quite safe, sir. He's with us in the police cells at the moment. Not for the first time either.'

'Really,' said Jerome.

'There's nothing you can do, sir, if you were thinking about trying. Probably best you keep out of it. He was caught in the act. Nothing missing here?'

'Anything that is mine is his to take.'

'Whatever you say, sir. But not everyone thinks the same as you.'

'I don't suppose they do.'

Jerome's first visit to Vince in prison was a revelation. He felt the need to share the experience.

'It was like a guided tour round a castle,' he confided one midnight to a couple of trollers from the park. 'I was escorted everywhere. I felt like royalty. Such an ordered life, monastic almost. And you could see into some of the cells. They were just sitting there – just, not doing anything – like a tableau vivant. But I bet things go on at night – sharing a cell with another young pretty. You could have a whale of a time. Even one of the officers gave me a long, hard look.'

Jerome never missed the monthly prison visit. On one visit he bumped into Vince's girlfriend – and on a later visit was introduced to a baby. He noted Vince had acquired a tattoo on his neck and nicotine stains on his fingers. His language had deteriorated and his political opinions become unsavoury.

It was not long before Vince was transferred to another prison, way up North and far more difficult to get to. By chance Jerome met someone in the park who had been born in that particular region and who had been only too glad to get away from it. Jerome smiled and took no notice. He convinced himself he had always wanted to go to that part of the country. 'It's no problem. It's only twenty miles from the nearest branch line station. I can get a taxi. I find a hotel and stay overnight. It would be like visiting relatives.'

Vince's first words to him were 'My girlfriend can't afford to visit all the way up here.'

Jerome was tempted to say 'Well, find another one

who can.' In the event he handed Vince a note of a fairly low denomination. 'I'd rather you gave it to her.'

'Yes, I think that's best, too,' said Vince, pocketing it.

Jerome never heard about the girlfriend again and when he asked politely the conversation was quickly changed.

'I'm getting out of here soon,' said Vince.

'That's marvellous. I'll have everything ready for you. It's still all as it was.'

Jerome brought back several trollers from the park and never failed to ask if they thought the bedroom needed redecorating. Most said yes, but no-one could decide on a colour. And nothing was done. Several weeks passed and a Prison Welfare Officer visited Jerome's house. She looked round and seemed impressed.

'I'm comfortably off,' said Jerome. 'Daddy left a bit and there's my pension.'

'Yes, but it's a set-up open to abuse. We'll need to monitor his progress.'

'What about mine?'

'It's up to you to look after yourself. Now, as to the neighbours. How might they react if they find Vince has just come out of jail?'

'However they bloody like. They don't come into the equation. He needs me, and I'm all he's got.'

'That's as may be – or not. His morale is low and he cannot cope with hassle. He needs Support in the Home Environment in the widest possible sense – in order to train for the Wonderful World of Work.'

When Jerome had a firm date for Vince's 'return' he was

galvanised into action. He had a king-size double bed installed. The old single was transferred to the spare bedroom. He filled the fridge with Vince's favourite junk food, and the cocktail cabinet with cans. On the day of the release Jerome gave Vince a set of keys on a key ring with his favourite cartoon animal.

Things began to go wrong at once.

'Can I have a Coming-Out Party?'

'Coming-Out?' said Jerome. 'Oh, you mean a release party? I suppose so.'

For the next few hours Vince was on the phone, talking at length to friends, and glowering when Jerome listened in. At the end of every call Vince gave Jerome's telephone number and address.

'Yeah. Come round. Any time. And phone. Reverse the charges. No problem.'

Within hours the house was full, some of the people far rougher than even Jerome would have knowingly entertained.

'I phoned for takeaways to be delivered,' said Vince, helpfully as he emptied the last can in the cocktail cabinet. 'I know you didn't have time to do any shopping.'

Jerome said nothing. He could have done with a drink.

'Well,' said Vince to his friends, 'now we're all nicely tanked up, I'll show you round. Come and look at the bedroom. Nice, isn't it? Wanna try it for size?' Two youths jumped on the bed with Vince. One of them turned to Jerome and said, 'You can go. And shut the door behind you.'

Next day, Jerome and Vince had a tremendous row, and

Vince flounced out. Several of Jerome's credit cards were missing. He phoned to stop all transactions.

'And he's taken Daddy's medals – perhaps he thinks they're Nazi heirlooms. Oh God,' he despaired, 'it's obvious he won't be looking after me in my extreme old age. But then I don't suppose I'll live as long as poor Daddy. He'll have the last laugh – from beyond the grave. I should have murdered him – but it's more likely someone'll murder me.'

A few days later Vince sloped back and Jerome, with infinite reluctance, let him in.

'I was going to have the lock changed.'

'Do you want your keys back?'

Jerome reproached him. 'Why? This to me? What did you hope to gain? Can't you see – I was the goose. I was the goose who would've laid the golden egg. You didn't have to pluck an illicit feather.'

'It wasn't me,' said Vince. 'It was one of my friends. Former friends. I don't see them anymore.'

For a time, things went well. No 'friends' came round, and the phone was disconnected. Then small items went missing. Nothing important or useful. Cuff links. And a tie-pin. Jerome put off making it an issue, thinking, 'Perhaps he likes these old-fashioned things. Perhaps he's never come across anything like them in his own life, and he's getting to know their value at long last. Or perhaps he even associates them in some way with me.'

Then he could hold back no longer. He raised the matter very tactfully.

'Perhaps you've lost them,' said Vince.

'No, I haven't lost them. I live here. I know where I keep things. I haven't moved them. I haven't used them recently. They've been in the same place for years. I am very particular.'

'Have you had anyone else round here?'

Jerome faltered. 'You ask me that?'

'What never during the time I was in prison? Did you go to their place every time? Or do it under the trees?'

Jerome was lost for words. 'I've been loyal to you. I would never do anything behind your back. You know that. And …' he paused and remembered what the Prison Welfare Officer had said about Vince having low morale and self-esteem. Jerome swallowed hard and said 'Why do you do yourself down in this way? Don't you think anyone could be loyal to you – through whatever circumstances?'

'Yes,' said Vince, getting up. 'But not you.'

Jerome wondered if there was much point contesting this. He felt like saying 'Yes, things were better when you were inside.'

He went upstairs and locked himself in the spare bedroom. There was a lot of noise below. He heard the front door slam. He gave Vince fifteen minutes to go – or rethink – and went downstairs to a deserted house.

'He's taken all his things, has he? What's he taken of mine?'

Everything seemed to be in its place.

Several weeks later Jerome was checking through his desk. 'Good Lord! He's taken Daddy's death certificate. What on earth for?'

He continued to check. 'Oh God! He's taken my birth certificate. It's almost …' Jerome felt a stab in the guts '… almost … as if … he's …'

Comrades

I DON'T REMEMBER THE CRASH ITSELF. Nor any screams. Or sirens. Only that a woman, a total stranger, died in my arms.

I was too stunned – by whatever it was that had happened – to call for help. A paramedic came up. I looked pleadingly into his eyes.

'Can't you help her?'

He shook his head.

Her head lolled on my chest and her glazing unfocused eyes stared up at me.

'Someone'll be back for the details,' the Medic said, and left.

I couldn't leave. I couldn't leave her. I was accountable, as never before, to a fellow human being. She had almost made an offering of herself, a gesture no-one could refuse.

The ambulances and emergency services began to arrive. All the space was needed. The other bodies were taken away. We were left till last. I heard someone say, 'They can't have been married long.'

I assumed her details were in her handbag. Should I open it? I wasn't sure I wanted to know. As it was, I felt like a looter.

I took a visiting card out of my wallet and wrote, 'So very sorry.' I tucked it into her hand and walked off in the general direction of home.

I had a frantic text message from the hanger-on who calls herself My Partner. I didn't reply – and unthinkingly turned into a side road, then turned right, and right again and again, then left and found myself back at the scene of the event. The whole area had been cordoned off. There were no ambulances, just hoists and cutting machines working by arc light. A crowd had gathered round the barriers, not relatives or friends, just ghouls, craning their necks, hovering round the film crews, moving forward every time a workman in protective gear arrived or left. There was nothing to see. The real players had moved on. The bodies had gone. She'd been taken. I had left. There was no point in staying.

I went straight home and looked at the report on television. An in-yer-face journalist was shrilling up-to-date snippets. 'Professional counsellors are on their way to help the bereaved. Even now as I stand here …'

The phone rang. It was an official from the scene.

'We got your details from your card. You didn't come to our Information Desk?'

'I didn't know there was one. Anyway, I've little to tell. I didn't know the lady.'

'I'm sure,' he said quietly, 'but we'd like to talk about it. Not just the woman. We need to know as much as we can. There's to be an Official Enquiry.'

'I can't remember much,' I protested. 'Anything at all – really.'

What have I to tell them? What's he accusing me of? I'd never noticed her until it happened. She must have been standing next to me on the train, gripping the handrail. I didn't touch her. If she'd bumped into me I'd've recoiled at the touch. Muttered an audible apology. Without meaning it. Possibly even mouthed an expletive.

'You're entitled to counselling help,' the voice said and rang off.

The woman who calls herself My Intended rushed in, thanked God, and smothered me with solicitous questions.

'The moment I heard I knew you'd been involved. I just knew.'

I didn't respond.

'I can quite understand you don't want to talk – yet.' She paused, presumably hoping I might blurt something out. 'Well, at least, have a bite to eat.'

I shook my head. The news bulletin said that information about the victims couldn't be released till all the bodies had been identified and the relatives informed.

I felt a pang of resentment. Please say she cannot be identified. Let her be a total unknown. Then I can give her an identity.

The phone rang again. My Erstwhile Partner answered it. 'It's a man. He wants to talk to you.'

It was her husband.

She did not live far away, quite near the train station after mine. I dreaded I'd see a more domestic background to her. The semi-detached was undistinguished, drab almost. The front garden was crazy-paved in a very tight-lipped way, with hardly any cement between the stones, several of which were buckling.

A middle-aged woman answered the door. She looked too young to be the mother or mother-in-law, possibly an older sister. I was shown into the front room and introduced to a horseshoe of relatives, all women, who sat on the sofa and armchairs, like items of furniture themselves.

'So,' one of them muttered. 'So. You were the last person to see her alive?'

They stared at me, as if I'd done something wrong. I didn't answer and looked round the room, wondering if the décor reflected her taste. I attributed all the kitsch to the husband, and the few good pieces to her. There was no other evidence of her existence but a small photo on the mantelpiece. He must have dominated her, stifled her with these relatives – his relatives, almost certainly not hers. How she must have hated him! She was looking for someone else. She did choose me. She did single me out. Do not pretend that In Extremis she didn't know her own mind.

'I'll get her husband,' said the slightly older woman. 'He's in the garden.'

They all hung their heads. At the thought of him grieving? What did he know of grief?

'He says he'd be pleased to see you. It might be better if you met – outside.'

She took me via a conservatory to the patio.

The husband was about my age, the same build, same colour hair. He had tired, swollen eyes. He looked drawn and cadaverous. I suspect he always looked like that, even before the accident.

'Thank you for coming,' he said. 'I just wanted to ask – if I might – if you don't mind, that is – well, not ask, no prepared questions, of course – really for you – to tell – to tell me – if …'

How could I not help despising him? He was unworthy of her. He hadn't protected her when she needed it. And it was me he seemed concerned for!

'It must've been very harrowing for you – not knowing this person – this … my wife.'

Was he implying she'd been forward and familiar? Wanton, deliberate even, in latching onto me as the last person she was ever to see?

'Bit surprised that she was … actually on that train.'

'Well, funnily enough, as it happens,' I said. 'I was on it only by chance. An announcement said there were delays and changes of platform. Yet there was a train waiting. I ignored it at first, but when I heard the whistle I instinctively ran – before even checking the destination. It turned out OK. I would normally have got a later one.'

'That's interesting,' he said. 'She usually went – earlier. It's a pity she wasn't on the usual one or …' He looked wistfully into the darkened garden. Perhaps he wanted to say 'Why couldn't it have been you who died?'

He shifted position and stared at me. 'In your arms, you say?'

I hadn't mentioned this. I assume he'd found out from

the paramedic or the Information Desk.

'She must've been standing very close to me,' I said. 'Then – before we reached the next station – it all happened.'

There was a long pause. I really wanted to say to him – I'd seen her from the start. So close, so tender, trusting, she came to my arms, without asking my permission – still less yours. She knew I'd accept. She was not a total stranger. She was in my arms long before she died.

'We had difficulty tracing you,' he said. 'The police said someone had disappeared without reporting properly.'

'Not exactly true. I left my card.'

'Oh, yes, indeed. So you did. I forgot. The police gave it to me.' He handed it back. 'I'm glad we met. Despite the circumstances.'

You mean despite the fact she died in my arms.

We shook hands.

So, he wants me to hand her back to his arms, does he? No, I will lay her gently in the earth.

'May I come to the funeral?' I asked.

He looked on the point of asking another question. I think it might have been – 'Did she call out my name? With her dying breath?'

The woman who keeps calling me Her Soul-Mate is getting on my nerves. I can't bear to touch her anymore. There's nothing there. She suggested I get counselling.

'Oh,' I said. 'You mean – talk about it, relive it, then get on the next crowded train?'

'I'm serious,' she insisted, and phoned to invite a counsellor to the house. He was there within the hour.

He looked like one of the ghouls.

'You're one of the lucky ones,' he assured me. 'Near the worst fatalities. Miraculously you survived. Not bereaved either. Nonetheless, we have enough counsellors to deal with your case as well. We'll need an hour for the first session, half an hour thereafter. It's a free service.'

His questions were endless. I sighed.

'This is for your Peace of Mind,' he said. 'Do you get flashbacks?'

'No.'

'What? None at all?'

'No. Not even of your questions.'

'My questions? Flashbacks of my questions? You mean my questions dwell in your mind? You hear them echo and resonate?'

'No. I think my hearing was damaged in the blast.'

'You can't hear what I'm saying! I hadn't thought of that possibility.'

He summoned my Would-be Partner. He spoke to her quite loudly. 'Typical. Seen it all before. In denial.' He patted her gently on the shoulder. 'Not to worry. I've no doubt my services will be called on again.'

From that moment till the day of the funeral was the most motivated time of my life. I conducted an investigation parallel to and surpassing the Official Tribunal. Once all the victims had been identified and the relatives informed, a list of names and photos appeared in the newspapers. She looked much younger in the photo. It helped me reconstruct her life on a more than conjectural basis. I photocopied all the reports; newsprint tends to turn brown. They became Exhibit A in my dossier, which I hoped soon to laminate.

Her name surprised me. The husband, so-called, had not mentioned it. He just said My Wife or She. And in a way I was grateful for this. A name ties one down. The surname – his name – was easily forgettable. Her first name was not the one I would have chosen for her. I have yet to decide how I'll address her.

Her age did not surprise me. She was my age. She could have been a lost twin. I checked the exact birth date in the Public Record Office. A few days separated us – even more a chance. Twins are Ordinary Fate. But we – we could have married, without incest.

The newspaper reports did not give the date she had married – not long ago I would have thought, but long enough for her to have regretted it. There were no children, which, with him as her husband, came as no surprise.

She had worked in the City. I checked the firm, and went to the wine bar nearest to the office. I spent lunchtime and evening eaves-dropping on her former colleagues, occasionally catching her name above the hubbub, trying to establish her rôle at work. I sat there for hours drinking, slowly. At closing time, I took the journey she'd have taken home.

I was careful not to be seen waiting outside her house at night. I had an unimpeded view through open windows, un-drawn curtains with the lights full on. The slightly older woman – the one I'd thought could be a sister –

seemed very close to the husband. In times of grief there is much hugging. But to that extent?

It was clear they were going through all the cupboards, having a turnout. The dustbins were full. I sifted through them, hoping for a keepsake. I was surprised they had chucked the newspapers. They couldn't have been keeping a scrapbook.

These investigations took up my waking hours. They helped put in perspective a recurrent dream, which even sleeping by day and waking at night could not dispel. It was a peaceful setting, in the eye of the storm. I drowned in the gaze of her eyes. They encompassed horizon after horizon. I couldn't close the lids. Even when I awoke from the dream, her eyes were still there, still open. Not even the coffin lid could close them. I wanted to look at her again in her entirety; uncorrupted, enhanced, fleshed out by the facts I'd learnt.

The funeral service was dull. The relatives I'd seen were there, plus some work colleagues from the wine bar, and several other people who seemed to think they had some right to attend. I could hardly wait for them all to go.

I stayed at the graveside all night. The flowers were beginning to fade. I pushed them on one side. The earth was fresh. I could easily have dislodged it. I sat at the end of the grave, like a faithful dog on a tomb top.

Her immediate family dropped in intermittently over the next few weeks. Their numbers soon dwindled, and their stay was progressively shorter. I, myself, was forced to return home on occasion.

The woman who says she is soon to be My Wife is becoming utterly insufferable. So is the doctor who gave me the certificate. So are the people from the job I had. But she is the worst. Every half hour she says, 'Are you alright?' She shows me pictures of wipe clean show-houses, travel brochures, bright sunny places, meals out. She seems to be wearing a new outfit every time I bother to look at her.

'It must've been awful. It could've been you. It was a miracle. Don't you see … Someone – Up There – wanted us to remain together.'

I laughed and almost replied … Someone – Down Here – had other plans.

I will not go to the cemetery on her birthday or the anniversary of her death. When the Investigating Tribunal finally reports the whole issue will be brought to life again, like Judgment Day itself. There'll be a resurgence of grief. The family will make a special pilgrimage.

I need not fear them. We are all beyond recognition now. They cannot take anything away from me. She is not in the coffin anyway. She is out there. Waiting for me. Looking like her double. Waiting for another calamity. I can meet her only in an extreme situation.

I frequent crowded, enclosed, vulnerable places – full trains, buses with standing room only, sale queues, capacity audiences.

Top of the Legs,
to you, too

I SPENT THE WHOLE DAY massaging my feet.
I'd been shown the correct technique by the
physiotherapist who, after much prodding with surgical
instruments, and a tsunami of technical language that I
didn't profess to understand, had finally got round to the
laying-on of hands.

'There will be pain,' he said. 'You can be sure of that.
But remember, always massage towards the heart so that
any inflammation will be carried away and not – as it were
– side-lined.'

With that, he began with my little toe, which wasn't
swollen and looked pretty bloodless. He slowly moved to
the other toes, and the instep and up to the ankle, and
then did the same for the other foot.

'Do that for half an hour three times a day till your
next appointment.'

The first day I was all eagerness and spent much longer
than he had suggested. The second day far less. The third
day hardly any time at all. And now I am making up for
lost time before the appointment tomorrow.

'A truly remarkable improvement,' he gasped when I took off my socks. 'Come walk towards me. And away, backwards. Your feet look ten years younger.' He gave me a tight hug. 'You've certainly worked hard. I admire a client who does exactly what I ask.' He rubbed his hands in glee. 'More on the ankle today. No, it's no good rolling up the trousers. They'll have to come right off.'

'But it's only my feet that are giving me trouble.'

He shook his head. 'The feet don't exist of themselves. They're a continuum of the leg. Susceptible to referred pain from the major joints. Not only that, the area between the ankle and the knee is the habitat of water retention, and the haunt of varicosity.' He gave me a deeply significant look, daring me to doubt or disagree. At the same time his fingers twitched eagerly, as if wanting to get down to business.

'Come,' he said. 'Let's gently massage, and knead those knotted muscles. Always towards the heart. Push to the heart. To the heart.'

I have to admit my legs felt a lot lighter, to say nothing of my feet which I hoped were now capable of any amount of nimble-footwork. I was more than happy to continue the exercises at home. Naturally I read up the anatomical background, and was amazed at the number of small bones and muscles in the feet. I am contemplating buying a pig's trotter to dissect. I have incidentally read up on a history of footwear, foot-fetishism, and learnt a few basic ballet steps.

I also anticipated what might be required of me at the next massage session. I was unwilling to remove my trousers again to reveal my underpants. I bought a pair of discreet shorts, neither floral nor khaki, and not beachwear, sporty, or pseudo-military but acceptable in the less energetic forms of folk-dancing. I tested that they did not bulk up too much under my trousers.

The physiotherapist's first words were, 'Knee to hip today.' Quickly followed by, 'Those'll have to come off.' He must have noticed my look of dismay and he added, 'No good being reticent with me. The hip is the largest joint in the body and the gluteus maximus the largest muscle. I'm here to help you, not to massage any mental fig-leaves.'

Reluctantly I took off the shorts – under which I had no underpants.

'That's better,' he said. 'If you're really worried, I'll close the blinds some more.'

He began to massage the area above the knee, and then more strongly the thighs. His thumb in particular made indentations into the upper thigh, rather like finger marks in putty. I noticed he was breathing more deeply, and so, I have to admit, was I.

'Look how the blood supply is having its effect. It's not going straight to the heart, but stopping for a while at that other seat of the affections. No knotted muscles there. Seems well-exercised. Well-massaged, I'll be bound.'

I was about to say, 'Yes, it certainly doesn't need your expertise' – or words to that effect – when he suddenly stopped.

'This is,' he said, 'where – with your permission – I'd

like to pause. I've always sought to educate and pass on the baton. Encourage things to be done at home. Exercises, self-massage, liberal applications to the affected area. Those are my aims and intentions which I observe even at the risk of invalidating my qualifications, and doing myself out of a job. And to prove my point I'd like to show you a range of products I've developed.'

He opened a cupboard door and took down a jar. 'Deep-heat miracle embrocation. Finger-rub application. Does the trick. And this,' – he held up an inflatable cushion – 'not just your usual inflatable doll. It has an accessory. This long tube is of specially reinforced inflatable plastic. As you lie on your stomach fucking into the cushion the tube can be inserted up the anus. The cushion contains pressurised gas, which expands when shaken and warmed, and ensures the tube expands as well. So that when you are pounding the pillow the tube inflates and pounds you. You can adjust it to your own needs. It is individually controlled and truly democratic. It aspires to a basic principle of Life – 'As you fuck, so are you fucked.'

'I fully realise that in developing these products I am potentially doing myself out of a job, as well as taking risks. But my main aim has always been to begin the process of education as early in life as possible. I have developed an exercise manual – to be used from the age of four onwards – for the ultimate in self-satisfaction. Which is, of course, auto-fellatio. But you must – like ballet dancers – start young and be supple. It can't, for instance, be left to your age.'

'No, I don't suppose it can,' I replied rather peeved.

By this time the blood supply which he had kindly pushed to the top extreme of my thighs had long since moved on – to the heart or wherever. Spleen possibly.

'I wonder,' he continued, 'if you, as one of my long-term patients and my greatest success story yet, would be so good as to sign a letter saying that you were not in the course of our long acquaintance molested by me. This is in case someone underage should ever complain. My whole aim is that they learn from me in order to do it themselves. Never that I do it to them. In this – as in all things – I am out of the loop, so to speak.'

More than so to speak, I thought to myself. 'But,' I added aloud, 'I will sign – for what it is worth.'

He thanked me profusely. 'Worth an enormous amount I can assure you in the Legal and Insurance circles I move in. You realise of course ...' – and he stared at me with one of his 'Don't you dare to doubt me or disagree with me' looks – 'that this concludes your course of treatment. There was, of course, never anything actually wrong with you at all.'

He seemed quite aerated to have made this offensive remark and had to sit down to steady himself. When he jumped up to see me to the door, I couldn't help noticing the squelch impression he had left on the chair. The flat end of a size 4 or 5 butt-plug, I would say.

Fly-trap

I WAS A BIOLOGIST, NOT A DOCTOR – but scientist enough to know there are times when bones have to be broken – a toe that needs straightening, a fracture that has badly set. Or, as in my case, a corpse stiffened too rigid to fit in a coffin. I had died awkwardly, with my limbs outstretched, angled at every joint, my fingers like scoops on a mechanical digger. I foresaw the problems a mortuary technician would face.

My demise had been caused by a combination of rocky outcrop and marshy ground. I was studying an insect-eating plant called the fly-trap. It grows only in boggy soil. I thought I'd more or less finished my researches, enough at least to produce a short interim report, when a vast new habitat became available; an uncharted area, un-ordnanced, and till recently out of bounds and used for military training. It was to be cleared of unexploded shells and barbed wire, then sold off and landscaped as a nature park. I determined to get in before that happened. However, permission was delayed until another scientist could – in effect – keep me company in that inhospitable region.

This was Louis. I'd met him once at a conference. His work overlapped with aspects of mine. Too simplistic to say he was primarily a botanist and I a lepidopterist – that was how the military authorities viewed our applications – but it was true our primary concerns were different.

Louis was interested in the life-cycle of the plants – how soon after 'blossoming' they could entrap insects, how many times each trap could operate, at what stage this capability was lost, the extent of the winter dormancy.

My own research had been mainly carried out in laboratories – on the sensitivity of insects to smell, and the effect it has on their flight patterns. Not just the change of speed and direction, but the wing angling, the slight aerial dance or drawing back, the marked drooping of the abdomen to slow the approach, and that odd kamikaze streak where some life forms put themselves in danger by flouting their own camouflage.

Louis and I hit it off. We weren't going to allow any possible overlap or rivalry in research to undermine work in such a prime location. We even talked of producing a book together. We set up a small camp, and arranged weekly supplies. We reckoned to spend the whole flowering season there.

Yet, from the outset, I sensed all was not well. Louis wasn't the sort of person I'd have chosen to work with. Professionally, in a laboratory, yes, or communicating by phone, post or at seminars. But not out in the field, by ourselves, close together. He was younger than me and had done well in his various postings, taking them all in his stride, unaware of his charm, oblivious of the effect he created. I soon adopted him as a rôle model, the person I wanted to be, with whom I'd like to exchange personalities. His presence rejuvenated me. I needed to

find what made him tick, then absorb the secret into my
bloodstream. I found myself imitating him, down to his
accent and mannerisms. An outsider would have noticed.
He didn't. It was not the plants and insects I found myself
studying – but him!

The terrain was varied, part rock, earth and bog. We
mapped out the solid causeways through the swampy
areas, and used little boulders that had fallen from the
rocky outcrops as stepping stones through the pools of
stagnant water. Neither of us had ever worked in an area
so rich in the plant we loved.

I made a tally of the numbers and species of insects
that had been trapped. This was possible even when the
traps were closed. Underneath were little charnel piles of
leg and wing – the so-called exoskeleton – that hadn't
been absorbed by the plant, or were outside the snap of
the 'jaws'. Sometimes, as I leant over to see the plants,
little pools of water reflected my face, green and
cadaverous.

I watched Louis flit unconcerned from one specimen
to another, totally absorbed in his work. He'd kneel
down, take notes, assess the age of each plant and with a
piece of dried grass test each open trap, timing the
reaction.

Further out into the boggy area, pond weed had grown
over the surface. The effect was of an inviting, well-mown
lawn. I scanned the area with binoculars and telephoto
lens. It wasn't easy to get a clear image. The early morning
mist soon gave way to midday haze. There were
occasional tufts of foliage. I reckoned the root systems
must be extensive or even interlace, feeding off

underwater plants and compacted moss.

There was one particular clump that resembled a fly-trap in outline, though it was much too large. I pointed it out to Louis, joking that perhaps in this unnaturally protected area the plants grew bigger, even lived longer.

He pooh-pooh-ed this but checked again when the air was clearer.

'What we really need,' I persisted, 'is a lens on a pole extension or duckboards. Or a cherry picker.'

He didn't respond. I added, 'Or to be lowered from a helicopter.'

He just snorted.

I shrugged. We both had our moons. Unco-ordinated. One of us on the wax, the other on the wane. One full, the other eclipsed, each with a different draw of the tides. The sun did not help, either. It made us irritable. Though it did have one saving grace; Louis just wore shorts and boots. I could barely take my eyes off him.

The sun came to dry the marsh. The water level went down. The clump of plants seemed closer. The uniform surface of the pond-weed was disturbed, as if the clump were floating, on patrol even.

'An optical illusion,' snapped Louis.

'I'm sure you're right,' I said and handed him the binoculars.

He went silent. 'Actually, yes, it is a fly-trap. Strange, so far out!' He shrugged. 'A one-off.'

Next day when the haze began to thin he took the binoculars before I had a chance to check the plant. It seemed to have moved further out.

'Much larger,' he said. 'And different. The hairs round

the edge are longer. Jointed, too. The trigger hairs are like spikes in an Iron Maiden. Extraordinary!'

There was nothing we could do. It was too far out. Louis seemed particularly frustrated, and kept putting his finger in his ear and jiggling around as if something was buzzing in his head.

One morning he came back dragging a large object. He'd found an old tree trunk – quite an achievement in a flat, windswept area. Also, a sheet of corrugated iron, a relic of war manoeuvres, horribly rusted the whole length of its parallels.

'You're not seriously thinking of . . . ?' He didn't reply and the more I warned him, albeit half-heartedly, the more determined he seemed.

He went to the farthest stepping stone and threw the sheet of corrugated iron as far as he could. It did not sink. He positioned the tree-trunk from the stone to the sheet. I stood on a stone behind, anxious to steady him. He edged along the trunk and tested the iron with a weighted bag.

'It's quite safe,' he assured me. 'Hardly notices. Not deep. Compacted roots. A slow sink. Easy to get out of. No problem if …' – he turned to hand me the bag – 'if … I diffuse my weight across the whole sheet.' He bent his knees and stretched out his arms in a diving position – and plunged. It was a brave thing to do. It paid off. He was winded but the sheet of iron did not give. He took out an extendable pole, one of the legs of a tripod, and stretched out to hook the clump of plants.

'They're quite different,' he called back. 'The hairs are

much longer. More than one joint, too. Each hair divides and at the end there are little suction pads. God, there's one over there that's got an enormous dragon-fly, big as a bird.'

He picked up a twig to test the reaction of an open fly-trap. As he stretched out his furthest, his body mass weighed down the central corrugations of the sheet of iron. It folded in half round him, spun like a crocodile spinning its victim, and disappeared below the surface.

I looked on aghast, mesmerised. I scrambled up an outcrop of rock and stared down on the scene. It looked no different. As if nothing had happened. There was nothing I could see. Nothing I could do. There was no-one near to help. What would be the point of shouting? Banging rocks together? Flashing a mirror in the sun? Setting alight tufts of dry glass?

I could believe what had happened. Yes, I could believe in it. In its way it was beautiful. I felt no sorrow or pity. I felt prompted to complete the event. I'd throw in his camera, his notes, his pile of clothes, all evidence of his existence. Then I'd throw in all my things – plunge in like he'd done. Join him.

I felt calm and elevated, breathed deeply, smiled and began to descend the outcrop. I must have trodden on some loose pebbles. I crashed onto the soft firm earth below. But I knew instinctively I'd never move again. Both legs and arms were broken; there was some protruding bone. Both wrists and both ankles had gone as well. A wheezing suggested broken ribs. The only movement I could make was to roll a few inches from side to side. My neck was contorted, but at least I overlooked the marsh Louis had sunk in.

I kept a vigil till the last. I dared not close my eyes or blink in case he materialised. The wisps of mist contorted into human shapes. In a delirium I fancied I rocked him in a final lullaby.

Slowly my broken limbs stiffened like the victims in a spider's web, or indeed dead spiders themselves, long legs, joints ossified at acute angles, half folded over and threaded through. Exposure to the elements soon hardened the skin, and sealed in the liquefying flesh and organs.

After my body was discovered there followed an extensive search for Louis. The military personnel spent their last – and probably most useful – session combing the area and dragging the marsh. Nothing was found. I was transferred to a laboratory, sampled, swabbed, syringed for any traces of Louis' body fluids or DNA. As if I was responsible for his disappearance! They even tested the contents of my stomach!

I was then unceremoniously carted away to the nearest undertaker's parlour, to join a line of coffins. I was placed on rods across the top of a coffin, rather in the way the coffin itself is supported on planks over the grave before being lowered on ropes. The undertaker passed the flat of his palm across my face, almost as a vicar might in a benediction. But my eyes stayed open. He tried again. Shrugged. Called out to his assistant 'You're going to have a job getting this one in.'

The apprentice emerged from behind the curtain of the changing rooms. He was young and athletic, and the more I looked at him the more he resembled Louis. I found him most attractive. And it was obvious the old undertaker did too. He fussed round, giving the apprentice the final instructions of the day. He stood too close, cast side-long glances, mock-slapped his wrist and said 'Oo! You'll have to go.' The apprentice didn't seem to mind, though I could envisage a stage when he might.

The undertaker pointed to the row of coffins. 'Seal those up. Ready for the morning.' He pointed to me. 'Make what you can of that. Leave it open. I'll check it first thing. Bye.'

The apprentice seemed much happier working on his own. I watched him flit from one open coffin to another, readjusting the contents, sealing the tight-fitting casket lids, wheeling them on their trolleys to the loading bays.

Finally, he came to me. My limbs stuck out at all angles. I could never be arranged neatly in a serene arms-crossed-on-the-chest pose. Even to get me into the coffin most of my bones needed to be broken.

I was happy for that to happen. And for the apprentice to do it. Under his protective gown he wore nothing but his underpants. Under his face-mask I sensed an angelic smile. And beneath his protective gloves were hands large and strong enough to break my brittle bones.

He stood looking down at me for some time, assessing the problem. He lifted me slightly to remove one of the supporting rods. His thumb punctured my side, and in doing so ruptured his glove. A drop of the liquid oozing out of me scorched his flesh. He unhurriedly took off the glove, washed his hand and put on another. He methodically dabbed the ooze that was accumulating out of my side. To staunch it he inserted what looked like a little cork. He forgot to clear some drips up on the floor.

I had not expected this level of consideration and gentleness. I thought he'd grab a hammer or axe and eagerly break the bones like some rough butcher's boy chopping meat or firewood. What a splendid young man! I have much to learn from him. Oh, to see the world through his clear eyes and healthy loins!

One by one he removed the supporting rods. He eased and massaged my bones, as a physiotherapist might a dislocated joint. Slowly, against its natural inclination, limb by limb was manoeuvred into the top width of the coffin. If, in getting one limb in, another sprang back to its former position the apprentice showed no impatience, and worked all the more diligently. Quite soon I was within the confines of the coffin, my arms and legs wedged just below the top ridge. My head and trunk could now be shuffled down.

He stopped, looked at his handiwork, and as an afterthought, stretched over to lay flat my wrist that was projecting like the plaintive gesture of an opening fern. He leaned over still further to ease me down into the coffin. As he adjusted position he stepped in a drip of the ooze and keeled over, compressing my rib-cage. His weight on me triggered a reaction. The limbs that he'd tucked into the side of the coffin sprang back to their former position of embrace; and ratchetted and clamped him in a python's lock. His ribcage cracked, his windpipe gutted and his own weight punctured my skin at innumerable points so that he sank into my liquefying innards.

The look on the poor boy's face told me of every little hurt he had ever sustained. The pain of a grazed knee as a toddler, a burn or cut or chastisement in childhood, a punch in a playground fight, a limb broken in sports. Every wound reopened and relived, and every humiliation fresh along its fault line.

Next morning the undertaker fumbled with his keys at the open door.

'You're early,' he called out. 'And you've done that coffin. Thought I told you to leave it open. Not that it matters. So where are you?'

I stepped out from behind the curtain of the changing room. He tried to avert his eyes. I'd taken off the protective robe and was naked but for my underpants and face mask. He'd not seen me like this before.

'Here I am,' I said. 'Here I am.'

Percy Propps

SOMETIMES PERCY WANTED to know us, and sometimes he didn't. One time he'd wave from across the road, and another he'd join us for a coffee and cake. Once, when we were discussing the problems of growing old, he appeared out of nowhere and took over the conversation.

'It really shouldn't be a problem,' he said. 'Not if you've established proper standards and correct style. It's certainly not a problem with me. I've always been known for my looks, deportment and snazzy dressing.'

There we are then, we thought. Get her. And we turned the pages of the freebie newspaper.

Another member of our group, Barry, arrived a little later, and said he'd just bumped into Percy.

'Do you know he didn't even say Hello? Just pointed to his forehead and said, "Those aren't age spots. They're freckles. I got them from my villa in the Bahamas." '

We all agreed Percy was far gone and needed humouring. We went back to the freebie newspaper. There was going to be another royal baby.

When Percy next deigned to join us Barry immediately began

'You know what's best for wrinkles, don't you?'

Percy pretended not to hear but leaned slightly forward.

'You'll never believe it,' said Barry. 'Fresh Spunk. Rubbed in. It'll tighten and flake off. Leaving your skin smooth. Got to be fresh though. From fit lads.'

Percy leaned back, with a revelatory expression. He was silent for a minute, before bursting out, 'What nonsense! What utter nonsense! What am I doing here listening to such drivel?'

'Oh, dear,' we all said, after he flaunced out.

'Do you think I offended him?' Barry asked.

We shrugged and read the freebie headlines. Hurricane Ida was approaching landfall.

The next time we saw Percy he was looking the worse for wear. He had a black eye, very smooth, not a wrinkle in it, streaked purple and orange, rather like a tropical sunset.

'I really must apologise for the walking stick. The doctor says I'll need one for at least another month. I had an accident. In my apartment, too. In the kitchen. I couldn't go in there for days. They say the worst accidents happen in the home, especially the kitchen.'

'And the toilets,' Barry added.

None of us ever expected to see Percy pushing a pram. He obviously wanted to be seen, but when we called out to him, he took no notice, and wheeled the pram down to the rival café where all the young mothers congregated.

'He's not going straight, is he? Making out he's a

grandfather?'

'What's he got in the pram?

Barry said, 'I once read of this woman who found a dead baby, and instead of telling the police, she had the baby mummified and put it in a pram and pretended it was her own.'

'What a truly stupid thing to do.'

'Not to her, it wasn't.'

Clarence walked round the block to see what was happening.

'Is he actually talking to them?' we asked.

'He's pretending the baby's asleep and mustn't be disturbed. He's just sitting there, while the mothers feed their babies. I think he's actually looking at their tits!'

Good God. That man is so sad!

We continued to meet mid-morning in the café. We were surprised when one of the lady regulars at the rival café approached us and asked, 'Excuse me. Do you know by chance of an old man? With a small pram?'

'Vaguely. He's not annoying you, is he?'

'No, he hasn't turned up for several days and we're worried about the baby.'

Don't be, we all wanted to say. It's not real.

'You wouldn't happen to know, would you, where he lives? So I can go and see if there's a for-sale notice outside. It'd be such a comfort to know he's moved on.'

We crumpled up! A comfort for us, too. A for-sale notice outside the dump he squats in? A skip full of his old shit, more like.

Last Throw

'FANCY A CHRISTMAS DRINK?'

Do I just! Magic words. I need to reward myself for all the hard work I've put in throughout the year. Pity the invitation came from Niall. Boring old fart.

'And afterwards,' he went on, 'we could troll down to that new club – well, new to you. I'm getting to know it rather well.'

'If we must.' I checked my diary. Christmas this year straddled a weekend, and so did the New Year. Plenty of time then, I thought, before committing myself to a date. I put off phoning him back.

'Leaving it a bit fine, aren't you?'

'Just want to break the ice, and dip in a toe. Can't we just have a drink locally?'

Niall insisted we go to the part of London that had come to be known as the Village, and check out the club he had adopted.

'Not telling you anything about it till we get there.'

We set out, muffled against the cold, almost in disguise. I'd not been to this area for years, indeed I'd deliberately steered clear since it had become so trendy, less exclusive and, as it were, on-tap. The whole area was being redeveloped, and the approach roads were a no-

man's land. The few remaining shops were closed and
shuttered, and most were fly-posted. All had notices.

CLOSING DOWN
OPENING SOON
WATCH THIS SPACE

It was difficult to tell which shops were about to go into
the boarding-up stage, and which ones were coming out.

Half way along, with its shutters still up, was a narrow-
fronted pawnbroker's. The display shelves were empty,
but still had sheets of lining paper, discoloured and at the
edges showing the rust marks of staples and drawing pins.
A large notice proclaimed

WE DO NOT KEEP MONEY
ON THE PREMISES.

Crouching in the entrance, opposite a corner full of leaves
the wind had blown in, was a beggar, young, male,
wrapped in a cloak, hood over his head, with cut-off
mittens. There was a hat beside him containing a few
coins.

He didn't look up, or ask for money. Without thinking
I tossed a couple of coins into the hat.

'Thank you, gentlemen. Hope you get a good shag
tonight.'

I didn't say anything to Niall till we turned the corner
and were out of earshot.

'Did you hear what he said?'

'Difficult not to. That's what comes of giving him
money.'

'Do you think he took us to be a couple?'

'What if he did? Doubt if his opinions or mine would
coincide on any subject. Why bother with the likes of

him? It's not far to the club now.'

He prattled on and on about the club. I half listened.
I was intrigued by the beggar. Nowadays they are
encouraged to be polite, and non-aggressive, not like the
old-style ones you could rely on for a threatening gesture
and a mouthful of abuse. A politer approach was thought
to yield more money. This beggar may have guessed what
we were up to. It was Friday night, and we were going in
a certain direction. But he had a welcome turn of phrase.
Nothing to get aerated about. He probably said the same
to everyone.

The club Niall so enthused about was not there
anymore. It had been replaced. By another club. New
name. New management.

'Good God,' Niall gasped. 'That was quick.'

'It's had a make-over,' I laughed.

'A refurbishment,' he corrected.

The façade was off-putting. Up front, cutting edge,
state of the art. It tried too hard. The welcome was
pressurised, reduced trial membership, cheap introduc-
tory offers.

THREE DRINKS FOR THE PRICE OF TWO.
Even the bouncer at the door gave the averted-eye smile
of the short-weight-giver. We dithered.

'Oh, come on,' Niall said. 'Nothing ventured ...'

Inside, was non-descript and wipe-clean, the sort of
half-hearted place you could spend an evening drinking,
ogling and getting nowhere. We bought drinks, which
were overpriced. We could not hear ourselves above the
thumping music. We got separated when we tried to find
the toilet.

The saving grace was that within minutes I was approached by someone half my age. My God, he was gorgeous, a delectable little number. Begged to be taken back. Just what I needed. So what if he turned out a one-night stand? I couldn't have handled more.

A few days later I phoned Niall and asked if he'd had any luck at the club. He said he hadn't. He never asked me if I had. I didn't choose to tell.

The following weekend I determined on a repeat visit, without him. I set off at the same time, wore the same clothes, and took the same route. The beggar-boy was in the pawnbroker's doorway as before. A fly-poster said

GRAND CLEARANCE
BARGAINS GALORE

There was nothing in the window to clear. It was much colder, and I gave the boy several large coins. In fact, I threw them in like dice, hoping for a winning number.

'Thank you, sir. Hope you get your leg over this weekend.'

Mm! Me, too! And as it happened, before I even reached the club, I met up with someone who was to grace my apartment the whole weekend. Tasty little number, far better than I had any right to expect. And not at all mercenary. Half way through proceedings he asked to pop out to the shops. I was surprised when he actually came back, the more so with a little present for me. How different from all those former pick-ups, who had turned nasty, demanded money, and threatened me the way tramps used to. I felt ten foot tall, chipper. Really like old times. Of course, it was a one-off. That suited me fine. I was glad I could still command attention.

Over the Christmas weekend I had unavoidable family commitments. I mucked in. It would have been churlish not to. There was little else to do. Most shops and places of entertainment were closed. I wondered vaguely what the beggar-boy might be doing. I hoped he was warm, well-fed and in good company.

A lot more was scheduled at the New Year. I couldn't bear another weekend cooped up. I resolved to get out. What I really wanted was to hear that beggar-boy say – I mulled over possible phrases – 'Thank you, sir. Hope your New Year starts off with a bonk.' That would do nicely. Or 'Hope you get it the whole year through, sir.' Yes, something along those lines would suit me fine. 'Whenever you're in the mood, sir.' Oh, yes. I like that a lot. He knows what to say, doesn't he? He can read my mind. I'm pretty sure he doesn't say things like that to everyone. Almost certainly I'm singled out. Next time I must stop and chat – just a few words, to start with.

I sorted the appropriate coins. £2 coins. Several of them. Notes would flutter, and not land where I wanted them to. But the coins I could lob into the hat and see if they were heads or tails. Or even clicked together as in a game of boules.

The whole world was out that evening. I dreaded I might bump into Niall. I dawdled as I approached the pawnbrokers. I waited till no-one else was around, pretending to look into some of the other shops which had just re-opened under new management. He wasn't there. The shop window was fully boarded and marked
VACANT
There was no way of telling its former use.

Had he been moved on? Temporarily. Had another tramp tried to barge into his patch? Perhaps he'd come into money? A rich benefactor had adopted him? No, more likely, he'd just nipped off, and would soon be back, like those notices on shop doors

GONE FOR LUNCH
WON'T BE LONG

What was the other one?

BACK IN FIVE MINUTES

You had to give them ten minutes, of course. I gave him much more. I walked round the block several times, checking the doorway. He never appeared.

And I never made the Village, or the club. I ended up in an all-night pub. I popped out every so often for the cool night air, and listened to the distant sounds of the New Year celebrations. Perhaps he was there, enjoying himself. I got almost as drunk as the revellers.

Dare I ask any of them if they'd seen him? Yes, I dared, but no, I didn't.

The area looked so different in the morning light. I couldn't force myself back there till it was dark again. Then every night I was there. At the same time, wearing the same clothes, taking the same route. Not just weekends, but every evening, and well into the New Year. I even thought of contacting Niall and asking if he knew anything. In fact, I was on the point of phoning him when by some telepathy the phone rang.

Did I really want to talk to Niall? What if it weren't him? But the boy? With a message for me. *I traced your number. Got somewhere warm you can invite me to?*

It was only Niall.

'Do you want to check out the Village again?' he asked. 'See if you can manage to get something this time? First time in a new place is always a disaster. You mustn't let it put you off.'

I made excuses. I didn't want to risk being seen again with the likes of him. Not in that area. We might be taken for a couple again. I had higher hopes. Higher. Much higher.

I didn't want to go on haunting in that area. Equally I didn't feel to give money to other beggars. I relocated, to the Piccadilly end of Bond Street ... to that sparkling cluster of shops, branches of internationally-famed jewellers. Not to go inside, but to stare at the window displays.

Each window is made smaller to highlight and protect the displays. Open-ended cubes are set on parapets, to form a proscenium, or to suggest a safe with an open door. At the back is a drop curtain, often made of glass, and the flooring always resembling a carpet or parquet. Curtains and drapes enclose the space, which is lit by footlights and spotlights.

Much of the jewellery is displayed – as it were – on dismembered parts. A featureless head, with a brow-band and medallion. A headless bosom-less trunk, with a necklace, or throat choker. An outstretched gloved hand, with a ring. A handless stump for a single bracelet or watch. A wrist up to the elbow for dangling bracelets. An oval cross-section of wrist to show a valuable watch strap.

There were tiers and staging, ladders, a swing and hammock, and a kind of double gibbet on which to hang ear-rings. Little velvet cushions, dimpled as the flab of an upper arm, showed off a watch or bracelet. There were sets of mini tables and chairs, miniature hampers and caskets, all overflowing, and half-unwrapped presents with the spotlight catching the peeping jewel. A ring was half sunk in a reflecting stand to complete the circle.

One window-display even had a perch for a thieving magpie, looking for anything shiny. A cocked head, a beady eye, and a purple sheen to its feathers. Knows what it's after. Won't be like a tramp and squabble over a piece of silver paper or a glistening gob of spit.

The jewellery twinkled invitingly, threatening to outlast all its owners. Its function and worth, self-evident. No maker's mark. No price. A case of – If you need to ask the price you can't afford it.

I was particularly taken by a cabinet, positioned in a narrow window alcove. One of the small side-lamps flickered erratically. Only for a nano-second. Yet it affected the shine on the gemstones. Turned them on and off. A smile momentarily became a frown. The faulty light was obvious only to the by-stander in the street, not to the staff inside.

This display had another attraction. The mirror at the back reflected not just the rear of the exhibit, and my ever-peering face, but often someone who seemed to be looking over my shoulder. Cute young men, faces half-masked. Perhaps too close for comfort. Did they assume I had the ready cash on me to buy them something? When I stepped aside and turned, they had gone. Yet I felt a presence nearby, something warm and protective.

Each evening, at closing time, the shop windows were emptied. In many cases the whole fitment, or at least the display stands, were lifted out into the shop. Or a grille, like a portcullis, came down, or a safety curtain. But in some windows, one, a shadow passed over the display. A secret panel in the drop curtain slid open and a pair of disembodied hands slipped through, the ends of the fingers gloved, in a reverse mitten. The fingers poised expectantly, like the snout of a blind mole emerging into the light.

Do you remember those old cameras? When a film got stuck inside? The assistant at the photographer's shop would put the camera into a black cloth bag, then put in his own hands, feel around, and extract the film, without any daylight ruining it. That's how it was at the jewellers. Not like the eager fingers of a tramp gathering and counting coins from a hat. But sensitive, infallibly accurate, fingers, locating each piece of jewellery, and touching at the crucial point, never the precious stone, never the dismembered body part, but the clasp or clip or thread.

How forlorn the body parts looked bereft of their function and finery. I longed to re-arrange and re-assemble them, give them life, and adorn them with jewels.

To whom did those elegant fingers belong? Whose hands were they that had plucked ripe fruit from the underside? Not surely the gross manager, with a small eye-glass stuck permanently in one of his piggy eyes. Nor any of the staff visible inside, nor the burley bouncer.

Rather to an unseen acrobat, gymnast, prestidigiteur, who would dance along pipes, and slip through keyholes. Who never left at closing time. Perhaps lived on site. Or was at least the last to leave, turning on all the alarm systems, and having to high-step and tip-toe to avoid breaking a circuit.

Perhaps other special precautions were required? A complete change of dress to avoid all suspicion? A downgrade from workaday clothes, or official uniforms? A total reversal of persona? Someone you would never dream of being a guardian of the jewels.

Yes, I think I will catch a glimpse of my man tonight. But where will this last wisp from the chimney materialise? Out the front would be too obvious. Through a back entrance, into a side street? Up roof ladders and fire escapes, ducking behind parapets? A silhouette dancing from balcony to balcony, crossing hand-over-hand along string courses, hand-below-hand down drain pipes? Or will he take the basement route, and come up a man-hole into the street?

It was dark enough to secrete myself in a doorway immediately opposite my favoured window. Leaves had accumulated in one corner, blown in by the wind. I drew my cloak round me, and pulled up my hood. If anyone passed by and looked in I was unfailingly polite.

Binkie and the Snowbirds

EXCUSE ME. Why are you staring at me like that? There's nothing wrong in looking good, is there? Haven't you ever seen a man wearing a bracelet before? New here, are you? Snowbird? Flown in for our winter? Well, we're hot all year round.

Oh, it's my dog you're looking at, is it? A lot of people do. Almost everyone round here has got a dog. A little dog. Wonderful ice-breakers. It's how we became such a tight-knit community. You can stroke it if you want. It won't bite. Can't you see? It's not real. Not anymore. It's stuffed. Runs on castors. A lot of people have their favourite dog stuffed. And then made up to look its best. My one's not actually my favourite. And that is quite unusual. There's a story behind it. Buy me a cocktail, and I'll tell you.

I got Binkie as a puppy. So I could train her. She didn't need it. From the start she had her own routines. She ended up planning my life! Always the same route for her walks. Always the same time. And always ending at this café. Binkie just loved it here. Ever the centre of attention. She showed up all the other dogs. Everyone made a fuss of her. She never went without. She had a really good life. All she ever wanted.

Not terribly adventurous perhaps. They say dogs walk three times as far as their owners. Binkie didn't. Most times when I let her off the leash she'd still trot along by my ankles, half the time expecting to be picked up and carried. It was the same routine every day. Out the apartment, down the stairs – she hated elevators – over to the greenwalk alongside the swamp, then on to the bridge, where we'd look down on the alligators. And I'd cuddle Binkie and say, 'Be a good girl. Or the crocs'll get you.' She knew I didn't mean it. 'You can't be too careful,' I said. Which was true. Because the alligators do come out – on the road you see them sometimes. They're no danger to humans. Adults, anyway. But they do take dogs. Quite frightening some of the stories you hear.

I actually thought of changing the route we took for our walk. Especially when building started on that apartment block overlooking the swamp. Too close for comfort for my liking. The apartments weren't cheap. They were advertised and sold before they were built. The dirt and disruption! And the thought of being spied on as you walked past with your dog. I tried another route, but Binkie wasn't having it. She was so set in her ways. The block got higher and higher, and some apartments were occupied before the garden surround had been properly landscaped. They just couldn't wait to get in and take over. Not likely to be the sort of people we'd want to know. Binkie and I hastened past the block and avoided eye contact. When we got to the bridge we'd studiously look at the swamp, and spot the alligators.

Well, one day, as we were hurrying past, I heard a peal of laughter. I thought it might be at my expense. I was not going to let that pass. I looked up and on the top floor, right in the picture window, was a couple, both young, both stripped to the waist, nice bodies, just fooling around. I have to admit they were the finest newcomers I'd seen that year. Take back all I said. Roll on the fresh meat. Made me feel younger just looking at them. They were so into each other, so pre-occupied they hadn't seen me. I couldn't take me eyes off them. Then they both waved, genuine, smiling. I thought, 'That's nice. Snowbirds fitting in so quickly.' I waved back. They tried to open the picture window, but they couldn't manage it and began tapping on the glass fit to break it – as if they were trying to get out, with a fire or something trapping their exit. I ran across the road to help. They started shaking their heads and pointing frantically. Then I realised.

They were warning me. I turned round and saw Binkie being tossed in the air by an alligator, and plunging headfirst down its open jaws. Before I could shout, 'Come back, that's my dog' the croc was underwater with hardly a ripple. Nothing surfaced. Not even a bubble. I ran to the bridge and looked both sides. There was nothing. It was so silent. I could hear my own sobs.

One of the regular dog-walkers saw me and ran up and I told him what had happened. He said, 'You've gotta get another dog. You mustn't let this put you off. It's like a car accident or a plane crash. You must get straight back in the driving seat. Get on the next scheduled flight wherever it's going. That's the only way. Promise me you won't leave it too long.'

I supposed this was right, but I didn't feel to do

anything immediately. A week or so later I forced myself to the local pet store. It's a very good one. A comprehensive range of dogs. Little dogs. I saw one there. The spitting image of Binkie. I couldn't believe my eyes. Almost as if she'd come back. Unfortunately, it was a He. But in everything else it could have been her. I just knew I had to have it. I didn't even ask the price. I said straightaway to the assistant, 'I want that one.' 'Certainly, sir,' he said. 'And is there anything else, sir.' 'Yes,' I said. 'Have it put to sleep and get it stuffed.'

I got the idea for the platform on castors from a lady friend. She had a dachshund, a sausage dog. I never liked them myself. Their back legs go. You can strap on a special trolley. Like a horse and cart, with the horse pulling its own back legs.

So, there we are. Things haven't changed. I still take the new Binkie for a walk. We're here every day about this time. Most of the regulars think it's the original Binkie. If they look too closely between its legs I say, 'She had a sex change just before she died.'

The only difference is the dog leash. I bought one of those retractable ones. It works on the same principle as a hoover cable, but much more powerful. I keep it at a short length to pull Binkie alongside me. But when we get to the greenwalk, in front of the new apartments, I take Binkie down to the water's edge and rush back to the sidewalk unthreading the leash. In no time the alligator comes out and heads straight for Binkie. I push the catch on the leash and Binkie shoots across the grass faster than ever a living dog could run. You should hear the castors clatter on the sidewalk. And the alligator – it's the same one, I know, they're very territorial – goes without. Serve it right. It'll come to regret what it did. It's already looking thinner.

I do this every day. Just to taunt it. And I like to think that the pair of Snowbirds are still looking out the apartment block. I couldn't live like that. Stuck inside, top floor, viewing the world out a picture window. Elevator permanently out of order. Pretty sure I saw one of them recently. Close up he was nothing. And much older than you'd think. Hardly worth a second glance.

Go on, pat him if you want. It'll cost you another cocktail. You don't wag your tail anymore, do you, darling? Don't suppose the alligator does either. What did you say your name was?

Mandorla

(The Story of a Substitute who wasn't Up-to-the Job)

THE BIRTH BLESSING FAIRY had spent untold years giving out the Fruits of Good Living.

'Unending, isn't it?' she moaned, as she gave out Nine Lives to every Cat and One Hymen to every Human Female. 'I need a break.' She decided on a half day's leave and left her Deputy in charge.

But because The Birth Blessing Fairy was a control freak, and had worked so hard in the past, her Deputy had never been given proper training.

Even before the Birth Blessing Fairy had left the office the Deputy called her back.

'I've made a terrible mistake.'

'What already?'

'Yes, I got confused. I gave the wrong sort of pussy nine lives. I've just given a girl-baby nine hymens.'

'God, this could wreak havoc.'

'But what about the pussy-cat I only gave one life to?'

'Fuck it.'

'It's a girl,' the midwife said, holding up the baby to the mother. 'I'm so glad for you. They're much less trouble than boys. At least to start with. See you again in thirteen years' time – when she starts breeding.'

'She's got almond eyes. Let's call her Mandorla.'

'Isn't she an angel?' everyone said.

'Yes,' said her mother, 'and once she's in bed she goes straight to sleep. No hanky-panky with her. She never cries out in the night.'

'She's so cuddly, too,' said one of the aunts. 'Just like a little kitten.'

And Mandorla's aunt bought her a kitten for her birthday. But it died. So did the replacement.

'We'll get her a china one for her bedside.'

Mandorla grew up a quiet and sensitive girl. She never cried however much strain was put on her.

'Doesn't she look dreadful?' her mother said to a neighbour. 'I wish she'd confide in me more. A son would have been a lot more fun.'

'Never mind. Perhaps she'll blossom out when she gets to secondary school. Some of the common girls will knock a corner or two off her.'

Mandorla was very shy and she stood aside from the other girls.

"Oo's she think she is?' a common girl asked her companions.

'Yeah,' they all demanded, rounding on Mandorla. "Oo d'yer think you are?'

Mandorla made no reply.

'What's up with 'er? Not all there.'

'You mean she IS all there,' laughed another girl. 'She wouldn't be so stuck up if she'd 'ad a bit stuck up. Eh?'

'She's thirteen and she's still a virgin.'
''Snothin' to be proud of.'
''Sno virtue in that!'
'It's turning 'er mad. She wants to get rid of it.'

That night Mandorla sobbed into her pillow. 'Why can't I be like other girls?' The feathers in the pillow were duck down and though they had been separated from the duck for many years they were still fully waterproofed. Mandorla's tears ran off them and off the edge of the bed. 'Oh, I can't go on like this. They laugh at me! I'll show them. I'll go one better.'

In the morning at school she tuned into some boy talk.

'I never fuck with a condom,' the leader boasted. 'I'm not worried about catching anything. Do you know why?'

'No,' said all the other boys.

'Do you want me to tell you?'

'Yes,' they all said.

'You see. It's 'cos I only fuck virgins. And never a second time. Good thinking, eh?'

'Great,' they all chorused.

'I've had more maidenheads than ...' he trailed off when he noticed Mandorla. 'Excuse me, lads, I've got to go.'

'Coming on a bit strong, aren't we?' he said to Mandorla. 'Standing there, ear-wagging. Making up for lost time, are we? No girl can say No to me for long. You'll get more than you bargained for.'

'Prove it,' she said.

He was getting all excited now. 'You're gonna let me then?'

'Is it in?' she cried.

'Right up your tight little …'

'Can't feel a thing.'

'I've popped her,' he said, withdrawing. 'The snootiest one in the class. Full house now. Except the teacher.'

'Was that it?' thought Mandorla. She shrugged. 'I suppose it's got possibilities.'

Next day Mandorla's form mistress asked to see her in private.

'There is a rumour going round that you've BEEN WITH that Awful Boy. I had hoped that at least one of my girls could keep away from That-Sort-of-Thing. It is true?'

'I can't say?'

'What do you mean, you can't say?'

Mandorla shrugged and shook her head. The mistress did not repeat the question.

'I'll just have to examine you then,' and she put Mandorla in position.

'It's perfectly normal down there, all intact. The same place, the same size. Not that any two are exactly the same, of course.'

'But it can't be there.'

'You sound as if you don't want it to be! If, as you say, you have had sex with a member, a member of the opposite sex, then it would appear, in the face of all medical history, saving only Our Blessed Lady, that a hymen has grown back again.'

She pulled out her finger.

'He said he'd broken it.'

'He would, wouldn't he? So he can boast he's had the only girl in class who resisted him. And you're pretending, too, just so you can be like the other girls. I've come across this sort of nonsense before.'

She strode to the door. 'Come in,' she said to the girls, eagerly waiting outside. 'Tell that young man he has no cause to boast. It is typical of him that he should want to harm the most vulnerable and sensitive of my girls. And it is understandable that this girl who is under pressure should play along with his domination. But it is not so. I have examined her. She remains the only one among you for whom I have any respect.'

'He wouldn't lie, Miss,' said a very forward girl. 'He doesn't need to. Not that you'd know.'

'Why you brazen little tart! Are you doubting me?'

'Miss, we don't want to doubt you,' said a humble girl. 'We all should have listened to what you said in class, then we would all have a Future-in-Life. But I know what men are like. And that boy wouldn't boast unless he'd done it. Can I check Mandorla, too?'

The teacher smiled at her. 'My dear, I knew you had a streak of goodness in you. If only you hadn't succumbed. Of course, you can test her. With or without a glove?'

'Teacher's right. It's still there. Wish mine was.'

Outside the girls talked among themselves.

'I don't think he's done it with half the girls he claims

to.'

'He's rotten to the core.'

'He's a liar. It's not Mandorla's fault that she lied, too. Like teacher said, we put her under pressure. She's vulnerable.'

'Yes, it's not 'er fault.'

'We should've taken more notice of teacher.'

And so they avoided the boy. He went into a sulk, while they attended classes and were very protective to Mandorla.

'It's long overdue – their change of heart,' Mandorla thought, 'but I don't feel bound by it. In fact, I don't even feel like going to school anymore.'

She couldn't sleep that night thinking about the possibilities.

'Why doesn't she go to sleep?' cried the Deputy Birth Blessing Fairy. 'I want to appear to her in a dream. And warn her that she's got a Special Gift.'

'Is that necessary?' asked the Birth Blessing Fairy Herself. 'I'd like to see what she can find out for herself.'

Next morning Mandorla spoke to some rough boys queueing outside the Job Centre. She told them she was a virgin.

'Not for much longer – with me around,' one of them said.

'Aw, come off it,' said another, taking Mandorla aside and confiding to her. 'This is how it goes, darling. It hurts the first time. Like having your tonsils out, or your appendix. They aren't really necessary anyway. So you might as well get rid of them. Or a tooth extraction. Hurts for a while – but you go on eating. A dentist is a kind of de-flowerer. So is a surgeon. I, myself, am a very skilled operator – in hymen extraction. I've dealt with hundreds of cases. I've got notes on them all. I don't deal with any other operations now. It's my speciality.'

'Get on with it, then,' said Mandorla. 'Or I'll die under the anaesthetic.'

'Put up a bit of resistance, will you? It makes it stiffer.'

'That's just an excuse. Are you gay underneath?'

'Sure, but what's that got to do with my dick or your fanny?'

'Not a lot,' she admitted.

Word got round about this episode, too.

'There's talk,' said Mandorla's mother, 'that you've been behaving badly with street boys.'

'Not so,' Mandorla said.

'Then you won't mind if Auntie tests you.'

'Not so,' Auntie reported. And Mandorla herself was more surprised than anyone.

That night the Deputy Birth Blessing Fairy waited for Mandorla to go to sleep. 'I've got my speech prepared for when she begins to dream. It goes like this. "You don't have to lose it now, you know. You can be experienced and keep it as a nice surprise for Prince Charming." '

'Oh,' said the Birth Blessing Fairy Herself, 'now I was going to say to her – "If you could enjoy the sex and still convince the world you were a virgin, then you'd have the best of both worlds. That's every girl's dream." '

'Mm!' thought Mandorla as she lay awake, 'I know it's fun being able to have it and – not get blamed for it. But till you actually lose it – no-one really admires you. And I don't want to be badly thought of. I wonder how many times I can go before losing it altogether? Let's find out.' As she stretched out on the bed planning what she would do she knocked the china kitten onto the floor.

Next day, she rushed down to the changing rooms of the local Rugby team. She pushed all the cheer leaders out the way. 'Let me be your mascot,' she cried. But the team went on drinking with their mates. 'What? Not even a quickie?'

So, she waited at the harbour gates for the fleet to dock. She elbowed her way to the front of the queue and watched the sailors come down the gang plank. Her heart fluttered. 'Some of those boys haven't seen a woman for over two and half years!'

'Nice try,' said the Birth Blessing Fairy. 'But if the fucks come all in one go – in a gang bang – then it only counts as one. It can't grow back that quick. We're only up to number three. Six more to go.'

Next morning Mandorla walked past a newsagents and saw the photo on the front of the tabloids. The headlines blurted 'Uncouple me, Nursie.' A couple had had sex on a crowded beach and the man had found he could not extricate himself.

'It must have been the hot weather,' he said later, 'and the excitement of all those spectators.'

'I pushed and pushed,' said the woman, 'harder than when I had my first pair of twins.'

'It could happen to anyone,' Nursie said later at a press conference. 'Though it's the first time in this hospital. Lots of swelling up after they die, of course. You can't imagine the number of cases we have in here of old stiffs stuck up their young pick-ups. My advice, after twenty years as a nurse (and considerably more on the job) is don't keep it in too long. It can cause damage.'

'Can it?' thought Mandorla. 'That's marvellous. The chances of a beach swelling may be remote, but …'

And off she went to the cardiac clinic. She told the duty sister 'I'm here on voluntary service. I'm a psychiatric social worker, specialising in counselling the over-eighties.'

'Well, don't excite them too much,' yawned the sister.

Mandorla danced up to the first bed and sang –

'Tell me, Doctor, won't you please,
    Is it love or heart disease?'

And five minutes after her first consultation she knew the answer – both.

'Let go,' pleaded Mandorla, 'it might kill you.'

'What a way to go,' the old man said.

'Don't say that. Just promise you won't die on me.'

'Why should I? What's it to you?'

'Well, if you must … No, no. I couldn't bear it.'

'Just let me do it. And I'll give you all the money you want.'

Money hadn't come into Mandorla's calculations before.

'OK. Die on me then,' she said invitingly.

But none of them did. However, the duty sister was amazed at the improvement in their blood pressure.

By now Mandorla was beginning to lose hope. She resigned herself. 'This is going to take longer than I thought. I might as well do it for money.'

She went to the Red Light District Job Centre to sign on.

'Speak through the grille,' said Madame. 'Do you have any Skills? Special Skills?'

'I'm a virgin.'

'ID, please.'

The other working girls were not happy with Mandorla's repeated claim that she was a virgin. It was not long before Madame had to intervene.

'You're causing problems. I appreciate that there are men who think that simply because they've deflowered – or claim to have deflowered – a girl that the girl is in some way their special property. In your case I've had two men in quick succession asking to book up with you again. In this Office we don't like our girls to develop long-term relationships. Once is long-term enough. Anyway, you've been getting extra tips, which you haven't declared on the appropriate forms. Your services are no longer required. You're on the streets. And don't think you can set up in business by yourself.'

And she down slammed the grille.

'Oh,' cried Mandorla. 'Can no man rid me of this hymen? It's all I ask. I only want men for their whatsits. I don't want the rest of them. I can happily do without the Body Attachment.'

And why not the whatsits as well? A substitute is as good as the 'real thing.'

Mandorla went to the sex shops, past the satin'n'frills and the leather'n'chains, down the back stairs to the toys.

'Why, this is just like a Nursery,' she exclaimed. 'I could play here for hours.'

She was amazed at the selection – sapling, tree-trunks, smooth bark and knobbly, some with imitation veins, like ivy keeping a crumbling pillar erect. Others streamlined, aerodynamically exaggerated and needing a battery inserted. Hydraulics, too. Mandorla inspected them all.

The shop assistant approached her, 'If Madam does not find what she is looking for here, then we do have more Out-the-Back.'

'Yes, please,' said Mandorla, following.

'Take this one, for example. It's particularly versatile. Not only can you choose the size and shape but it fixes by suction onto the wall so you can choose the height and angle. You can use it as an exerciser, or rest on it like a shooting stick. Either facing the wall or with your back to it. Mirrors add to the spectacle.'

'Yes,' said Mandorla, 'that's the one for me. I'll take two.'

'They are not cheap.'

'Money's no object.'

Back home in the bathroom Mandorla adjusted the suction pad, the height and the angle, stood on tip-toe and let her legs give way. She repeated this a hundred times. There was no trace of blood, but her ankles swelled up.

'There's nothing I can do.' She gave a resigned post-menopausal look and raised her eyes to heaven.

'I've lost count of the times now,' said the Birth Blessing Fairy. 'All those sailors only counted as one. And a dildo shouldn't count at all. But if it Duz the Biz then ... who knows?'

Mandorla began to despair. As she walked along the High Street at night she noticed that a wide ravine had opened. The edge was tempting. She shied away and then returned to look down. She almost convinced herself that she was weightless and that the rocks below were as soft as pillows. The gulf seemed to come and go, turn corners and double back. On the far side she sensed a shadowy figure, half emerging from the dark and looking her way with penetrating eyes. Mandorla hurried on, studiously not looking either side, certain she was on the right path. The ravine narrowed and she stopped to investigate. She could see the shadow more clearly now. It was sometimes a woman and sometimes a cat. It acquired a voice, and made kissing noises as if calling a pet. 'I know that voice.' It was like her old school mistress.

'Do you like the sound of me?' the voice called out. 'You can see me as well, if you like. Here I am' – and a slinky woman in furs appeared, elegant hands holding together the coat lapels, a breast peeping out, the face hidden in the high collar.

'Here's all of me. I contain everyone – female, male, adult, child, beast. I can slink and purr and seduce. Or I can growl and leap over to get you. I can turn into a bull and charge. I can slip in and out of my robe. How do you like me now? And now? And now?'

Mandorla said nothing.

'What's this? Playing hard to get? What's wrong? Do you think I've got something missing? I don't think I have, but to please you …' She strapped on an enormous dildo, much bigger than the ones Mandorla had seen in the sex shops. 'Think it suits me? This can solve your problems, eh?'

Mandorla said nothing.

'Are you coming over? This gap only exists in your mind. It's only a little gap. We can walk till it closes completely.'

'I've been walking long enough.'

'Then I'll jump over.'

The moment she said that Mandorla noticed the gap widen. The Catwoman laughed.

'What are obstacles for – but to overcome? I can jump that easily. Do you think I wouldn't risk it for you? Just watch this. We cats have nine lives. Me – I'm pussy all through!'

Catwoman slunk along the edge, sizing up the gap. She made a trial run then stopped. She laughed confidently as she crouched before her leap. She hadn't reckoned with the massive dildo, the extra weight and the bobbing effect. The rubber tip hit the far wall of the ravine a split second before Catwoman's fingers were able to get a grip. She bounced back a few feet, before falling …

Mandorla looked away – and covered her eyes. She felt a wrench in her guts and a slight trickle of blood.

'Hello, Mandorla,' said another voice. It was a girl with a pram. 'Don't you recognise me? I was in your class. We regret what we said to you, and what we did to ourselves. We didn't mean to drive you away. Did you really go into a nunnery, like teacher said? This is my baby. I called her Mandorla. I want her to be like you.'

'That's beautiful. But it's too late now. The damage has been done.'

'What do you mean …?'

'I've lost it.'

'It? Oh, that!' said the girl and shrugged. 'So what?'

'No,' said Mandorla and held her head. 'Up here, I've lost it.'

'I can't understand you, Mandorla. You always were a hard nut to crack.'

Mandorla walked on.

In desperation Mandorla thought of self-mutilation. She wondered about the boundary between 'self-abuse' and self-harm. She remembered excuses that women were said to make when they lost 'it.' Pathetic stories, all of them. She was not going to jump off branches onto passing horses, gallop bareback over rocky terrain or slide down banisters without removing the post at the end. Or go ski-ing and aim a tree trunk in her crutch. No, but she rather wished all those years ago the rocking horse in the Nursery had done the trick. It would have saved so much trouble now. And her mother would have comforted her, and confided.

Mandorla was going down fast now. Nearly there, she thought. And just in time for her consultation with Earth Mother.

'Good whatever-time-of-day-it-is-above-ground,' said the frail old lady.

'It's Eternal Night, Mother.'

'Bad as that, is it, dear? Then come in and tell me your story – if you must. Try and surprise me – if you can.'

Earth Mother listened to Mandorla's story. 'I am ALL-WISE but I've never heard of your problem before. A cherry like granite, yes. But not a self-replacing one.'

'Can you help me?' pleaded Mandorla. 'No riddles and nothing too cryptic.'

'Listen carefully. Know this. You can only lose your virginity from the inside – not when the willie goes in, but when a baby comes out. It is not the act of being fucked, but of giving birth, that marks the true end of virginity. Now that's not what you want to hear, I'll be bound.'

Mandorla went away, much chastened.

'This is beginning to sound a bit like a Moral,' said the

Birth Blessing Fairy. 'Trust bloody Earth Mother to come up with something like that.'

'But it all fits in, doesn't it?' said the Deputy. 'Mandorla's only got one left. She's in the same position as any other girl now. I can't believe it's going to happen at last. She's been more desperate to get rid of that hymen than an unwanted pregnancy. Come to think of it, do you think an abortion would do the trick as well?'

'It's her decision how this story ends. But she'd have to get pregnant first.'

Mandorla had come to believe that she could only lose her hymen when a baby came out. She decided to bypass a man going in. She took a deposit from a Sperm Bank and did whatever had to be done herself.

'Whoopee!' cried the Deputy. 'It's taken. The problem's solved. My mistake's been put right at last. Can I try again?' she asked. 'Nine Lives to the cats – that's right, isn't it? And one Hymen to the Human babies?'

'Oh, alright,' said the Birth Blessing Fairy Herself. 'But make sure it's a girl baby first.'

Mandorla's baby was a boy. The baby had a cherry birthmark on its head. 'Don't worry about that,' the midwife said. 'Hair will cover it.'

'So glad it's a boy,' the Deputy Birth Blessing Fairy said. 'I don't think she would have fully lost her virginity with a female baby. It takes a male to do the trick.'

'What utter crap you do talk,' said the Birth Blessing

Fairy Herself.

'Does that mean I can't have another go, after all?' asked the Deputy.

'No, it means that in order to reduce my workload – and this is how the whole episode began – I will give out the Birth Blessing Gifts to the girl babies. And you can concentrate on giving out the Nine Lives to the cats. Before they become extinct.'

'What if I were to give the cats nine hymens?'

'Just don't. Please. Just don't.'

Parenting

FATHER: Come in, son. And Happy Birthday. Your Mummy and I would like to talk to you. When we first had you, all those years ago, we agreed that we would ...

MOTHER: We certainly did.

FATHER: And now the time has come.

MOTHER: It's about your body, my dear.

FATHER: You're ripe.

MOTHER: Daddy's prepared all the relevant documents.

FATHER: I surely have. To start with – here's a photo of your Mummy and me on our wedding day. It was taken in the church porch. As you can see your Mummy was still a virgin. But not for long after that, eh? And this is the photo of your Mummy the next morning. Can you spot the difference?

MOTHER: We didn't try for a baby till about a year afterwards. Daddy didn't wear a condom that night. That's one of those things in this glossy catalogue. You can keep it. And here's a photo of your Daddy not wearing a condom. He does look eager to become a father, doesn't he?

FATHER: We also delayed having you so we could save up for a camcorder. And all the trimmings. Including a timing device.

MOTHER: Daddy set it up, and leapt into position just as

the tape started. Here's what happened the night you were conceived.

FATHER: Ho! Ho! That didn't take long, did it? As you can see we waited till summer so we didn't need any bed clothes to keep us warm.

MOTHER: A few weeks later, and we got the good news.

FATHER: Here's Mummy holding her tummy in delight. Look at that sparkle in her eyes.

MOTHER: Yes. The next pictures are very special for me. They are X-rays of your development inside me. You did grow quickly, and move around a lot.

FATHER: In no time at all it was back to the camcorder. Your Mummy wanted to give birth to you in a swimming pool, but we had to settle on the maternity ward. Here comes your head. And then the rest of you. Look, you can see it's a boy. It gets clearer once the afterbirth has been washed off.

MOTHER: All the nurses said you were the most beautiful baby they'd ever seen. We took photos of you every day for the first three months.

FATHER: Your mother was so proud of you. She took you to all the local cake shops so she could show you off, being breast-fed in public.

MOTHER: Here's one of you asleep, with my left nipple half in your mouth. Can see what you preferred

FATHER: Looks like you're going be a bit of a titman, just like your old Dad.

MOTHER: Here's one of you at your circumcision. Before ...

FATHER: ... and after.

MOTHER: We took photos of you at every important time.

FATHER: School uniform.

MOTHER: Sports Day. Holidays.

FATHER: First pair of long trousers. I expect you can remember some of these.

MOTHER: And one, of course, on every birthday.

FATHER: It really is a wonderful photographic record of every stage of your development to maturity.

MOTHER: We will, of course, leave this chronicle to you in our will. So you can show your children.

BOTH: Our grandchildren.

FATHER: It will a) inform them of the basic facts ...

MOTHER: b) help them overcome shyness and inhibitions ...

FATHER: ... and most of all c) respect the importance of handing down such skills.

MOTHER: Now, if there's anything you want to ask us please feel free. We'll always be here, keeping an eye on you. I think your Daddy's got a word of advice for you.

FATHER: I have indeed. It might be an idea to make a record of yourself to hand down to your children. Unfortunately our record – good though it is – is not complete.

MOTHER: Daddy and I forgot to photo the bloodied sheet.

FATHER: A once-in-a-lifetime chance lost forever.

MOTHER: Also ... there's nothing about the time before your Daddy and I met.

FATHER: Well, to make sure you don't make the same mistakes we made your Mummy has kindly said she'll be happy to film you having your first masturbation.

MOTHER: Daddy doesn't need to do that sort of thing anymore, but he might be able to remember a few helpful tips for you. So he'd like to be in the room as well. And ...

FATHER: ... we were wondering ...

MOTHER: ... if it would be more a family occasion if your Daddy and I made love, so as to give you the necessary stimulus.

FATHER: Then you could show your appreciation ...

MOTHER: ... and come all over us.

BOTH: It would mean so much to know that our only son had turned out alright.

The Card Sender

WHAT'S UP?' ASKED PETER.

He was hovering behind me, pretending not to be interested in the contents of the letter I was reading. He often did this when he recognised the handwriting of a former lover.

'Oh, nothing. Well, there is actually. It's from Barnabas.'

'Oh, is it, now?'

'You know it is. Read from here down.'

It is a source of regret that I am unable to invite you to my wedding.

'His wedding?'

'So it says. First I heard of it.'

I'm sure you will want to wish us – that is Barnabas and Mary – well, and will be thinking of us at 3pm. on Saturday 14th September. Should you wish to send us a present the forwarding address is …

'What a bloody cheek!' Peter went off alarming – as he often did. He had replaced Barnabas as my lover, and was ever-eager to run him down.

'*Should you wish to send* … No home address. Just a forwarding address – for the present!'

It was odd, hurtful and frankly out of character for Barnabas to be so secretive. He was usually open, inquisitive and full of himself, rather like Peter, in fact. He looked a bit like him, too.

I wondered what the woman was like. ' – *that is Barnabas and* … *Martha.*' No, beg her pardon Mary. Not that it mattered. Barnabas tended not to call people by their names, but by endearments. Dear, Darling, My Other Half, sometimes even My Better Half. How long before he'd call her The Wife? I've always hated that expression – when the word THE is made more possessive than My, and more institutionalised, the only possible one, the taken-for-granted one.

Peter was about to embark again but I stopped him.

'Now that he's about to be married he's no danger to you. Why keep on?'

'Aren't you even offended?'

'Intrigued.'

'He should have told you. So soon after splitting up. Think it's on the rebound? Well, do you?' he repeated. 'Or even a shotgun wedding?'

'I can't honestly believe that.'

'Why not?'

'Because in the three years we were together he showed no more inclination to take the so-called dominant role – than you have.'

This ended the conversation and no further mention was made of the subject until Christmas.

The card was a very religious one. It was signed by Barnabas and Mary.

> *Looking forward to meeting you. Have heard so much about you.*

The handwriting was not Barnabas's, nor was the signature, as Peter was not slow to point out.

'She obviously does all the organising in the household.'

'We can't know that.'

'Shall I put it on the tree with the other cards? In pride of place? Or chuck it?'

I was about to hand it to him when I noticed a message on the other side – again in her handwriting

> *Thou shalt not spill thy seed.*

'What's up?' asked Peter.

'Nothing important. I'll chuck it.'

'Aren't you going to send them a card?'

'I've only got a forwarding address.'

Thou shalt not spill thy seed. I wonder how much Barnabas has told her. And how much she has guessed or surmised. And why – after being married several months – should she still be interested?

My birthday comes just after New Year. I wish it didn't.
It is one celebration after another. I received a card from
Barnabas and Mary. Inside was a piece of writing paper
and in her writing the message –

> *I hope the conjunction of Christmas, the New Year
> and your birthday will give you the strength to turn
> over a new leaf.*

'Well,' I laughed. 'It never has done before.' I turned the
card over to see if there was a further message. This time
she had written their home address, presumably a hint for
my not having sent a Christmas card. Damn! Now I
suppose I'll have to send Barnabas a birthday card. I
checked the date. It was in May.

There was, however, an intervening communication. I
always go on holiday in March – not from choice, but
because it fits in with my job. I have been going in March
for several years. Barnabas came with me on three
occasions. This year was the first time with Peter. When
we returned there was a card waiting for us. It read –

> *We'll be in your area next week. Will drop in.*

'Oh, God, what's the date?'
    'Over two weeks ago,' said Peter.
    'Thank God for that.'
    'Isn't it typical inviting themselves round here – but
not inviting you to their wedding.'
    'Married couples can be like that. They assume single

people need them so much that they can drop in as they please.'

'But why isn't there a note saying they called and found us out?'

'That's a point. She wouldn't have missed an opportunity to send a card.'

'Do you think they actually came?'

It was rather strange. Barnabas must have known we would be away this time of year. Perhaps he'd told her and she was writing without his knowledge.

In May I duly sent Barnabas a birthday card. Four days later I received a thank-you card from Mary.

'A thank-you card for a birthday card?' shrieked Peter. 'For a present, yes. But not for a card. It wasn't even HER birthday, either.'

> *We were most grateful for the card you sent Barnabas. I thought the picture on the card and the poem inside were quite delightful. I always read the poem. Some people don't.*

I'm sure I hadn't when I bought the card. Even if I had it couldn't have been worse than the quotation she added to the back of the card –

> *Thou shalt not lie with another man.*

There was no doubting the implication of that. I felt now I had to show Peter and tell him about the other cryptic messages.

'I should've told you before. But I didn't know how long it was going to go on for.'

'I understand. I only wish I could understand this woman. She's determined to let you know – she knows, isn't she?'

'Knows what?'

'Exactly.' He paused. 'And what's more, she's dividing the year up neatly.'

'That's true. You think she'll keep up the pressure?'

We both shrugged. We were tempted to ignore the whole thing but instead we agreed to confide in a close friend of mine, Randolph. Peter, who sees everyone as a threat, isn't very keen on him. It's true that years ago Randolph was a bit of a loose cannon. But he can be very helpful. He's now deeply into psycho-babble and keeps threatening to do a part-time counselling course. We showed him the cards, and after the initial hilarity and disbelief we settled down to a serious discussion.

'There are lots of women,' began Randolph, 'who like our sort – simply because they don't feel threatened.'

'Yes,' yawned Peter. 'They're called fag-hags. Tell us something we don't know.'

'Hold on. There are also some women who want to get married – and for one reason or another – haven't done so. Perhaps the opportunity has not arisen – '

' – or they're just plain ugly,' cut in Peter.

'Barnabas would never have made that remark,' I rebuked.

' – and,' continued Randolph, 'when the opportunity

does arise – even with a person they suspect is gay – they would rather take the risk – and it is a risk – than stay "on the shelf." '

'It's a risk for the man, too, Randolph,' interrupted Peter, adding 'as you must know yourself.' He gave me a look as much as to say 'Would Barnabas have said that?' I frowned. 'Oops! Sorry. Do go on.'

'I was just going to observe that – as late converts they will be extra eager to make the set-up work, stress family life, religion, morality and, of course, cut the links with former friends.'

'But surely this is the point,' said Peter. 'She is not cutting the links. She is writing to me on every pretext. And it is she who is doing the writing.'

Randolph shrugged. 'Perhaps she wants to convert you.'

'Which is quite uncalled for as I pose no threat to her.'

'Granted,' said Randolph, 'but she has managed, by whatever means, not only to find a husband, Barnabas, but to change his sexuality. This must give her an enormous boost. A successful mission accomplished. Now that she's proved one person can be 'won over' she must believe others can as well.'

'Which makes it a form of seduction? Or flirting.'

'That is actually,' mulled Randolph, 'a very perceptive remark.'

'Bet you wish you'd made it,' smiled Peter and added, 'Let's change the subject. I really can't feel sympathy for her.'

'No,' said Randolph, 'but I think it's good to try to understand where an opposite viewpoint is coming from.

Specially as you'll almost certainly be hearing from her
again.'

And he was right. The next communication was a change
of address card. Underneath was written –

> *We needed a larger place. We want to start a family.*
> *Why don't YOU settle down? It CAN be done.*

The quotation on the back was inevitably

> *Be fruitful and multiply.*

'Well,' said Peter. 'She's certainly using her success with
Barnabus to encourage you.'

 'She needn't bother.' I threw the card and address
away. I was not going to make contact and only hoped
she made no more.

A month later another card arrived. It read –

> *Is everything alright? This is to confirm our new*
> *address. We thought you might have lost it as we did*
> *not get a card wishing us a happy move. It was also*
> *our first wedding anniversary last week. If there is*
> *anything we can do to help please let us know.*

We showed the card to Randolph.

 'Don't you think it's a cheek?' I said. 'Why should I
send an anniversary card to them when I wasn't even
invited to the wedding!'

'Well, she couldn't invite you before she'd got her man in the bag. Now she has, she's making amends – albeit on her own terms.'

'Why? I'm not after Barnabas. I would have written to him if I was. It was me who turned him out.'

'Perhaps she's trying to tell you she's found qualities in Barnabas you never discovered.'

'Pooh!' said Peter. 'And do you suppose there'll be any more cards?'

'Bound to be. Could go on for ages.'

Despite Randolph's prediction – and I was getting rather fed up with his knowingness – there were no cards for a long time.

'She must have got the message,' said Peter.

'I'll believe it if we get through Christmas and my birthday unscathed.'

We did. It was amazing. We sent no cards and received none. We rejoiced too soon. There was a card when we returned from our March holiday. It read –

> *We're not having any success trying for a family. It is a great tragedy. We have both been for hospital checks. There should really be no problem. It is some time since we started trying and since we heard from you. Things seemed to go much better when you wrote.*

'I can't recall I ever did. Anyhow, Randolph, what's your verdict on that one?'

'She thinks you've put a jinx on her. That you still have

some power over Barnabas.'

'He might well wish he was back here. But that's none of my doing.'

'Tell me,' said Randolph. 'Can Barnabas – do it?'

'When I knew him – over two years ago – he always left that side of things to me. But there is no reason to suppose he can't – or that he is any less fertile than ...'

'No, indeed.'

'Will I be receiving ...?'

'Why ask? She'll write again.'

And he was right, of course. Damn him! But this time it was a letter, firmly sealed.

> *You have always been Barnabas's friend though you have not met for some time. Lately we have both been very sad. I know you would wish to correct the situation. After long discussions we have both agreed that you should give me a baby.*

'Just like that,' laughed Peter. 'And to be named after you as well? Insist on that.'

'Be serious, Peter.'

'Why should I be? She's now suggesting adultery with a man she's condemned for being gay.'

'There's actually some logic in her position,' said Randolph.

'Is there?' said Peter, not bothering to enquire further. He turned to me. 'What quotation are you going to use in your reply? "Thou shalt not commit adultery" '?

'No,' I said. 'I was thinking of something for myself.

'Thou shalt not fuck another's man's wife, especially if you've already fucked the husband.'"

'I like it,' laughed Peter. 'Why not go one better? Tell Barnabas to leave the house. She's never met you and we could send someone else round there instead? It could even be me. She's never seen me. They don't even know I exist.'

'Don't they?' asked Randolph, surprised. 'I assumed … That puts things …'

'Don't,' I begged.

I wrote back at once. It took me about ten minutes to think up a couple of lines.

'Let's see,' said Peter.

I handed it to him. 'You'll have to sign it as well.'

> *I'm sorry to learn about your sadness. But stable relationships can be maintained without children, as Peter and I have discovered.*

'Yes,' nodded Randolph. 'That should stop her writing any more cards.'

And he was right. We never heard from her again. And we didn't see so much of Randolph either.

Family Matters

MY PARENTS NEVER TOLD ME the Facts of Life. I learnt them by watching my mother and father have sex together. It was a bit like when they had rows, and told me to leave the room. I always listened at the keyhole, and when the row was over my father never failed to put his finger to his lips and say 'Shh! Keep it in the family.' Later I listened and looked from the security of their bedroom wardrobe. I assumed at first that they'd be experts at it, but after a while I was tempted to intervene and say 'Wouldn't it be better if you did this? Why don't you try that?' I would have been happy to join them and act as therapist. I'm sure they would have had fewer rows.

Something happened, and they didn't want me at home any more, and I was unceremoniously shunted out. I managed to be taken in by a large family as the boyfriend of the youngest daughter. There were many other daughters and brothers and dozens of cousins as well as a few steps and adoptees. And I remembered what my father had said 'Keep it in the family.' I got through the steps and adoptees in record time and was soon fucking the cousins. That's what cousins are for. And not long after I was into the sisters. One of the brothers obliged, and I began thinking about the mother.

They all seemed quite happy with this. 'You've got enough to go round,' they said. 'Just where did you learn your technique?' I always gave a 'comes-natural' shrug. But it set me thinking – back to my early experiences with my real family. The time when my elder sister said she'd drop her knickers and show me everything if I first dropped my pants. Well, I did and she didn't. Bitch. And there was the time when my elder brother began playing around with me, nothing penetrative, but it set me off and I was soon up him, and he put his finger to his lips and said 'Shh! Keep it in the family.' Or the time when I opened the bathroom door, which my mother had forgotten to lock, and there she was stark naked. I wasn't breastfed, and had never seen her tits before. I wanted to see more and was tempted to push her back in and lock the door from the inside.

The thing I really regret is never seeing my father's dick close to. I always wonder if it's bigger than mine, and how mine will be at his age, the staying power, the frequency, the amount, the length of load shot, and the sperm count. I've often wondered how big my son's dick will be. I'm still not sure if dick size comes from the genes of the father's side or from the mother's side, or a combination of the both. To be honest I've never thought before in terms of checking out my grandfathers'. They're both dead and buried, so I don't suppose they'd mind.

The Moon of Morollo

I TURNED THE FINAL PAGE AND READ –

'Moronding's Quest was done. He placed the faceted crystal in the rock cavity and restored equilibrium to the planet. Now the Moon of Morollo would shine again. And the Sacred Herons would nest by the Lake of QuigingLoops.'

This ends Part One of the Space-Time Chronicle: Dimension 4. If you enjoyed this Series why not try the Parallel Sequence called …

Called what? The name was missing! The bottom of the page had been torn. Deliberately? By the last reader? As a piece of wanton vandalism? No, more probably to make a roach. Or possibly a book-mark, though the burnt and neatly-folded piece of silver foil stuck at the end of the first chapter could have served just as well.

When I began my addiction I made a rule only to read the titles in strict order. However, a change in circumstances is forcing me to read whatever I can obtain. In some Series I have only read the even numbers. In other Series, the odds. Most only as far as the penultimate volume.

Perhaps there never is a conclusion to these Series. The Out-of-this-World struggle between Good and Evil is not one-off, but ongoing. That is what our Authorities say, too – and the prison chaplain agrees and extends it to what he calls the Inner Struggle.

'You'll like it here,' they said, they still being the Authorities, when I first arrived. 'It's a parallel society – a mini universe. It's got everything, and spins in its own orbit.'

I was not sure what to say.

'You are lucky,' they were later to add. 'You do not have to share. You're alone for your own protection. You are a vulnerable person. Both 'Inside' and 'On-the-Out'.'

If this is true then I am not sure why it should be. The Authorities accept I had never committed any 'crime' before. And they admit I'll never re-offend. Indeed, they say I can never re-offend. The offence I committed can never be committed again. Not by me. It's a crime that can only happen to the same person once – such as matricide, patricide or suicide. It's not repeatable – even if I wished to re-offend. In this sense, I'm no threat to anyone. Yet, they say, no-one 'Inside' or 'On-the-Out' will ever forgive, or let me forget. I must always be kept separate.

I cannot remember doing whatever it is I was supposed to have done, which makes it all the more difficult for me to protest my innocence. But they – the Law Givers, that is, the Enforcers, Interpreters, both Defence and Prosecution – all said there was evidence,

tangible and irrefutable, at the scene of the crime linking
'Me' with 'It.' Irrevocably. Indissolubly. Seemingly to the
very extent that my surname may now be used to identify
the particular crime I committed. Both as a noun and a
verb. Thus, giving me a form of linguistic immortality
which I never sought.

It does not matter. I would not look forward to being
released. Nor do I object to being used for their experi-
ments. I am not unhappy. I live in my pod, which is small,
compact with everything to hand, like a well-stocked
travelling case. Nothing is more than an arm's length
away – the food hatch, the light switch and the alarm
button. There is no wasted energy. In fact, there is such a
conservation of physical energy that I can by a mental
leap actually leave my body and look down on myself in
the pod and convince myself I am truly the centre of
operations.

Sometimes I feel I am lying on heavy water. I cannot
sink, but heave-to from side to side and stretch my arms
from shore to shore. Occasionally there are radio
transmissions from outside. As we get further from Earth
small service-craft dock alongside the pod to support me
in my long journey. There is much noise when the craft
connects, and not just the metallic clatter. The robot
attendants have a vocalese of their own.

Food is put through the air lock. I lie on the floor and
lean forward to collect it. The food is pre-digested. The
meat is hashed and the potatoes mashed, though sometimes they are both cut into cubes. A slightly yellow
version of the potatoes is probably diced swede. The peas
and beans are mushed. The greens are overcooked and

separate into slime, liquid and transparent stalk. The plates and the cutlery are plastic. The knives don't need to be sharp. The bread is sliced – and soggy. My fingers gather at it, rolling it into shapes and pellets, which I leave to dry. I don't complain. It's no worse than food served on commercial air flights. And we are so much further from earth. I use this word in reference to the soil, as well as to the planet of that name.

My main concern is that the shuttle provides the sustenance I long for, the nectar of The Sequences. At first, I was supplied regularly with the next title in whichever Series I was reading. Soon I did not receive the titles I had requested, but titles from other Series and even then in the wrong sequence. I sent them back and with fresh demands. Time and again. Then to satisfy my needs I was told I could go to the Book Reserve to check for myself.

Rigid safety and security guidelines were applied when I left the pod and 'walked outside.' It was vital I did not become detached, or I would float in Space forever. I was therefore put in protective clothing and chained at the wrists and ankles, and led from the pod under escort.

I saw several other travellers detached from their pods. They are easily recognised. They move uniformly, often in groups, and in strict formation.

I found the Book Reserve confusing. Sagas, Cycles, Chronicles, Sequences, Series, spinning off in all directions, one begetting another like a family tree. Yet I refused to be deflected, and insisted on extra time. I have always been methodical, and a slow reader. When a link is missing, I search for it. If I cannot find it after repeated searches I do not give up. I might even try to conjure it up and create it.

Eventually I found the title I was looking for, by chance, and way out of place on the shelves. Was it hiding from me? Or had some miscreant deliberately mis-shelved it? Either way I was destined to find it. The first volume of the new Series, parallel and follow-on, the dust-jacket in keeping with the old Series, and the names of the characters the same. And to clinch it, on the fly-leaf was the familiar, comforting map of Morollo!

It is like a hand-drawn escape map. The mountains resemble circumflex accents, and the forest of fir trees runic script. The Lake in the Sky is clearly marked at the highest point of the mountains, and the forest runs down to the shores of the Sea of the Moon. This was where Rhlimn first sang the Wish-Song that was eventually to become the anthem of the United Tribes of Mrothwolq, in their fight against the inhabitants of the Wild-Distant No-Land.

The blurb told of a development I could never have guessed. That Morollo has acquired a second moon! I have no doubt it is shining at this moment, though equally I am sure it will soon be the object of some enchanted devilment – perhaps a rogue meteorite that the Forces of Good have not been able to keep in check. I headed straight back to the pod to read the outcome.

However, something happened on the return voyage. Some form of in-transit attack. I tried to steer my course without stopping. I had to swerve to avoid being hit by debris, in particular those sensitive tangential bits, the feelers and antennae, that fly off when capsules go into their final irreversible spin. Seemingly there was only just time to get me back to a smaller pod. I was warned the journey time would now be longer.

No problem. I had the right book in the Series and settled down to read. It was slow going, and bore little relation to the blurb. I double-checked the details on the dust-cover against the details on the title page. They were different. I had the right cover and the wrong book.

I rang the alarm bell. Time and time again. I tried to explain the situation. I demanded another expedition to the Book Reserve. This was refused outright. 'Then you get me the book.' The request was not actually refused. Nothing happened. Everything went quiet. The craft dockings became less and the food scanter.

I persisted. I repeated the details and was told the title did not exist. I had made a mistake. I was told the supply had dried up. This I could not accept. I cannot believe there would be a sudden cessation, after so much had been forthcoming. I know there are many authors who write under four or five different names. They worked incessantly, fired and guided by the same spirit. My theory is that they are all one person, with alternative names for the Supreme Creative Force. All are One. This being so it cannot be that the Production of the Word would ever cease. There will always be scribes who till the end of time will chronicle the Happenings.

I have explained this a dozen times to all levels of the Authorities. No response. Silence makes my mind race on possibilities. Have the supplies been redirected to other pods, which I know are out there, though I cannot see them?

In despair I tear the book to shreds. And only when I reassemble it to form the next title in the Series do I realise the true situation. Morollo has acquired a Third Moon! Which I know for certain will turn out to be the biggest of the moons. It will have no phases. Will always be full. Can never be eclipsed. Not only that, the other two moons will orbit round it, in preference to the planet. Indeed, the planet itself will orbit this newest and greatest moon.

The Third Moon has now of necessity become the object of my long journey. My pod has changed direction. And the Third Moon is also moving towards me. We are exerting a gravitational pull on each other.

All external contacts and supplies have ceased. Yet I know everything I do in this pod is monitored. There are microphones and cameras taping me from all angles and at all times. Scientists need to analyse this data for future explorations. Everything is important to them, a disturbed sleep pattern, a minute deviation from the norm, a sneeze even.

Anything I do is significant, and of value. Yet my innermost thoughts, my true intentions, cannot be divined. I need to shout those out, loud, above the sound of the engine. Night is best, when the brain races faster. Yet every time I begin to shout there is a banging from outside. I shout louder. And still the noise continues. If anything, it gets worse.

Does whoever or whatever is making this contrary noise not realise I am seeking a moon as yet unverified or mapped, and known only to myself? One that could well be inhabited? I am preserving and extending the world of the Sagas and the Mighty Legends, central to human experience. Am I not fashioning a Creation Myth, which will be the foundation of a new religion, possibly even to be named after me?

It is quiet now. I scratch on the wall. There is little space left. I've designed a shorthand which, like hieroglyphs, includes pictorial elements. The map has changed — it is deforested, the mountains levelled, and the sea has receded in one area and flooded another. I have tried to mark some of the distant Galopp-stations.

Occasionally I've had to re-use space. This does not matter as there are certain elliptical elements in the story. It is all one story really, which can be told in a thousand different ways. But the telling must never cease.

I no longer write with a pen. At least not with the ink. That ran out some time ago. The metal tip can still scratch into the softer joints of the pod wall. Even fingernails can make a lasting impression.

Tidings

'JUST LISTEN TO HER,' Mr Townsend said. 'Singing along with the carols.'

Once in Royal David's city,

'She loves Christmas, doesn't she?' added his wife.
  'So she should. It's a time for children.'

Lived a mother and her child,

'She actually sings very nicely. You've got to admit she's very talented – musically.'

Jesus was that mother mild
Mary was that little child.

'Yes. That was lovely, too. Don't think the words were quite right.'
  'No, but the rhythm … and pitch.'
  'True. She understands the music, yes. But what about the meaning of the words? To say nothing of the story behind them. Do you think there's some sort of dissociation? Or dislocation, dysfunction, evidence of dyslexia, here?'

'Oh. Please. She's got enough wrong with her already. Don't let's find any more.'

'I think we ought to check it out, though,' said Mr Townsend. 'For our own peace of mind.'

They contacted Maria's headmistress at the special school.

'I am so glad you came. I have long found Maria a – well, we don't use the word problem, but a … challenge. Who is stretching our resources at a time when … She's no trouble or anything. And completely harmless. But she doesn't seem to pick up on things. Slow on the uptake.'

'I see. And can you suggest anything?'

'Well, I had thought of contacting you, about a session or two at that new clinic. You may well have heard of it. It's run by Everest Education. Quite outstanding. New concepts and initiatives. A radical new slant on remedial and rehab.'

'Thank you so much. We'd be grateful if you could.'

'I thought you'd warm to that. In fact, I checked in advance. Good thing I did. Only one slot left. Late Wednesday afternoon.'

'But that's Maria's music lesson. She likes that.'

'I daresay she does,' said the headmistress.

'And she's very good at it, too.'

'Yes, I daresay she is. In fact, I've heard she's the best in the class, but we mustn't let that stand in the way of her getting specialist help. Music won't get her a job. She'll never become an effective economic unit if that's all she likes. She's got to know all about the world outside.'

Maria was sad at having to miss her music lessons. She moped for a while. Then her parents were told she would need even more sessions at the new clinic. She was taken away from the school classes for gymnastics, where she was showing an aptitude for ballet. She later missed out on the drama class, where she loved reading poetry out loud.

'No problem,' said the headmistress. 'Not to worry. She's not losing out on the core curriculum. Just the frills. They won't broaden her outlook. She desperately needs current awareness training. That'll get her a job.'

Maria became very quiet. She never sang to herself. Yet she seemed more attentive and looked intently at the things around her. Sometimes she stared at an object for hours, her brow screwed up. She hardly said anything. Then after a few weeks at the new clinic she muttered, apropos of nothing, 'Than kyou.'

Her parents were not sure what they were being thanked for. They assumed it was for having arranged the sessions at the clinic. Once Maria had gone to bed, they discussed it further, but came to no conclusion.

'Oh, well. Whatever the reason it never hurts, does it? A show of gratitude. They're teaching her some good things at this new clinic. Long may it continue.'

When she went to bed the next night Maria hovered in the doorway and said

'Than kyou.' She paused and added. 'Than kyou, for turning off the light when you leave the room. It saves on finite resources.'

'Yes, dear. I'm sure it does. I try to do that anyway. To save on the electric bill.'

Maria's parents looked at each other and shrugged.

'Goodnight, dear.'

Later in the week Maria stood framed in the kitchen doorway.

'Than kyou. Than kyou, for using the green recycling bag I left by the sink.'

'Oh, you put it there, did you, darling? I picked it up as the first thing I could lay my hands on.'

'Than kyou. You have shown care and consideration for the environment.'

'Yes, dear. I'm sure you're right. Well, I've done in the kitchen now, and it's time to go into the front room. Daddy should've finished whatever it was he was doing by now. We can all watch The News together. I don't expect you'll want to miss that, will you?'

The main item of news concerned a cabinet minister accused of incompetence, policy change and embezzlement.

'Oh God. Not another one,' shouted Maria's father. 'If I had my way he'd be kicked out and prevented from holding office ever again.'

'Than kyou,' Maria said. 'Than kyou for not saying "Shoot the Bastard." '

'That's just what I was going to say. And if you hadn't been here I would've done.'

Maria got up to go. 'We must respect everyone,

whatever their opinions.' And without saying anymore she went to bed.

Her father snorted. 'Respect everyone's opinions? But he's only a bloody politician. When did they ever respect ours? Is this what they've been teaching her at that damn clinic?'

'I know what you mean,' agreed his wife. 'I'm a bit worried, too. I didn't tell you, but I found her in the kitchen the other day with a magnifying glass looking at the label on the bottle of the washing-up liquid. She said 'Thank you for not buying anything containing … I can't remember the name of the chemical. It was about a mile long. She had it off pat.'

'Oh, what have we let ourselves in for? It was much better when she just sang to herself. She was particularly good at wordless songs. There must be plenty where the words hardly matter.'

'You don't think this new clinic might have damaged her musical abilities?'

'Let's hope not. And let's hope her old school classes are still going. Do you think she'd be happier back there?'

'Yes, I'm sure she would. Much, much happier. And I know we would.'

They paused as they heard a noise from Maria's bedroom. It was a familiar word, being sung. 'Than kyou.'

Weeks later, after Maria had resumed her music classes, they heard her singing again.

Jingle Bells, Jingle Bells,
Jingle all the way.
Old MacDonald had a farm
On a Green Hill far away.

Whispering Campaigns

THE BLOOD RAN DOWN HIS FACE. It felt cool in the night air. It took the same fixed route, obeyed gravity and dripped off.

Something inside him had taken control, calmed and numbed him. He viewed himself from above, as he walked rather than ran, hearing without panic the shouts behind.

The sequence of events had been confused. The world had ceased to be familiar. Everything had become physical, practical, above all tactical.

And it was all tactics, wasn't it? Or failure of them on his part? Taking the wrong turning, getting cornered, not singling out the leader. Even at their age they understood tactics.

The taunts he'd heard often enough – faggot, poofter. That was as far as it had ever gone. Realising that the worst was about to happen had been strangely enervating. The mugging was over in seconds, and was not as bad as he'd feared. In fact, he felt slightly virtuous, almost high. He wanted to tell everyone, boast, lie, make himself the hero of the situation, but knew this was the last thing he could do. He took the long route back, avoiding everyone. As he reached home a fear and heaviness crystallised and concentrated his mind.

The implications were worse than the incident itself. Only one thing was important. Not, why did they do it? Not, who were they? Not, why him? Not even, what damage had been done? But simply – what will they say at work?

Work was a primary concern and contact. Adam took his job seriously. Even the chatter in the staffroom was a call to the bar of history. He could get the muggers out of his mind easily enough, but not his work colleagues. When he closed his front door and leaned back on it to collect himself, there they were waiting for him, just as they waited for him every morning in the staffroom. He could have faced them if he'd been the office boy, but when you're nominally in charge then old scores can be settled by personal comments.

Yes, and there was an expert at doing just that, wasn't there? Settling scores, and undermining authority were her specialities. Remembering things about people years on. Never giving anyone a second chance. Mounting whispering campaigns. Good old Mrs Taplin, Hilda Taplin. She was the one who'd cause him trouble. Hadn't she caused enough already?

He'd always tried to lead two distinct existences, home life and work life. This was not possible with Mrs Taplin. She spilled over from one to the other. She was the only member of staff whom, as it were, he 'took home with him.' He could cope with the others. They had their commitments. They didn't dwell on other people's lives. They worked for money, and they'd retire as soon as they could. She was the problem. She'd be the one officiating over the proceedings, leading the hounds. He could visualise the situation.

But not quite. He couldn't visualise her. There was nothing physical about her that registered. She was a heard object – a sharp tongue with body attachment.

He went into the bedroom, without turning on the light, or looking in the mirror. Sounds were more important now, above all the sound of her voice.

All her outlook – indeed all her brain pattern – came out in glib phrases, fired like barbs in all directions. She had to voice her opinion on everything. She could never say 'I just don't know enough about the subject.' She'd intervene as if she were an expert called upon to give an authoritative, definitive judgment. She always had to have the last word. There was no letting up. Each phrase, each triumphant phrase, outdid everyone else, admitted of no further discussion, banged down like a card in a game of Snap.

The phrases buzzed in his throbbing head. A favourite was 'I can imagine' – it was used in reply to events she couldn't possibly have known the first thing about. Then there was – 'You don't have to tell me. No-one knows that better than I do' – which served as a rebuke to anyone who dared suggest they might know more about a situation than she did. 'It's often the way' – 'I'm not surprised' – 'What else did you expect?' all proved she'd foreseen events. 'Oh, don't talk to me about ...' meant she was fully conversant with a problem and had heard so much about it that she'd no longer tolerate mention of it. 'I know exactly what you mean' – always came as an interruption, when someone had paused, perhaps trying hard to find suitable words for a sensitive situation. On the very rare occasions when she was obliged to agree with something she'd take over and claim 'Yes, this is IT, isn't it? I've been saying THIS for years.'

And how she exaggerated! She would have pronounced exclamation marks if she could. She made adjectives into adverbs. Anyone else would have said 'a bloody nuisance', 'utter chaos', 'sheer madness' or 'dire straits', but she said 'It was absolutely bloody, believe me, it was sheer, it was too utter for words, it was absolutely dire.' 'Absolutely' was her favourite word, though 'categorically' and 'totally' and 'utterly' weren't far behind.

And the way she counted! It was on the basis of one, two, three, then a gap to ten thousand. A crowd began with two people, a mob with three. Any more was a riot. She could manage one illegal immigrant. She might even sympathise with the odd refugee or two, but any number above that was 'an absolute flood, a sheer inundation.'

If you tried to stand up to this onslaught it was taken amiss, as Adam had recently discovered. There'd been a staff room disagreement. Hilda had been moaning about the crime figures and the sentences passed in the courts.

'Things won't get better till we bring back hanging.'

Adam had heard her say this many times before and let it pass. The subject was an old favourite in debating societies. Everyone knew the pros and cons, and no-one changed their minds. Yet he felt for that once he couldn't let her remark go unchallenged. Firmly and politely he put over the opposing arguments. She listened and said –

'Very interesting. Wait till something nasty happens

where you live. Even to you! I know what I'd do if I were in charge.'

She meant, of course, in charge of running the country. But before she could go on Adam had countered, confusing the phrase –

'Thank God, then, you're not in charge – and never likely to be.'

He'd used the emotive phrase 'in charge' in the sense of 'in charge at work'; his work authority against her private opinions.

Next day very publicly she got back at him. She'd taken a phone call and the caller said he'd been cut off and had earlier been talking to a man.

'You were talking to a man? Are you sure? Well, here's no-one of that description here. Unless you mean our Mister Adam. But he's not just a man,' and she added in hallowed tones, 'He's IN CHARGE of the WHOLE office.'

It was mildly amusing, Adam supposed. The staff had smiled. It wasn't perhaps a remark to get worked up over.

More disconcerting was perhaps what she didn't say. When she went through her list of prejudices – social workers, blacks, Asians, unmarried others, etc – she always omitted his particular grouping. It was odd that she'd list every other target possible without going for a full-house. Was this uncommon tact on her part? Surely not! The minute he left the room he was convinced she'd complete the list.

So what? He wasn't the only one who found her difficult. The other staff were resigned to her attitude. 'You'll never change her. Why try? Switch off. Let it all flood past.' Adam wished he could. It was easier to do that when he was at work, with his mind occupied. But now, in the middle of the night …

He looked at the clock. It was too late to phone any of his friends. He doubted, anyway, whether they'd be much comfort. They all had their own mugging stories; they wouldn't listen to his. He could imagine them coming out with the type of phrases that would've earned the approval of Hilda. 'Not surprised. What do you expect, the life you lead? Lucky it hasn't happened before, the amount of time you spend at it.' No, his friends would be no help. In a situation like this you were alone and in the dark.

Or – as now – in front of the mirror. He looked at his eye. A truly fine specimen. No story could be made up about being drunk and walking into a tree or lamp-post. It could only have come from a punch, so accurately placed that the eye swelled equally above and below. It was rather fetching. He'd always looked a second time at men with black eyes. The boy who punched him had talent.

Still, he wished the eye was invisible. Why couldn't his work colleagues see it, but ignore it? Was that an unreasonable request? How often had he clocked the love bites on their necks, and said nothing.

So, what explanation should he offer? Surely, a question of tactics. Hadn't he already established that with the muggers? They'd taught him a lot. The quick ordeal was preferable to the interrogation to come. The muggers had been strangers. They hadn't meant it personally. Hilda undoubtedly would.

He must have ready answers for likely questions, and as rich an armoury of phrases as Hilda's. He couldn't tell the truth. That would be pointless. He hardly remembered the actual sequence of events. He hated having to lie. He wanted to rise above it in the dissociated way that had happened when he was mugged.

He might begin 'Thank you for your concern. Do you mind not asking? I'm rather fed up going over it.' This was a stalling tactic, a promise to say later, an indication he'd already told a lot of people, closer people.

He could even say – 'I won't bore you with the details.' He quite liked that phrase. It implied 'I'm not going to tell you anyway. I don't feel bound to justify myself.'

Or he could kill it stone-dead by putting it in a bland sociological context. 'These things happen, though not as often as is made out. The figures are not really going up. It's just that the incidents are now reported. Like accidents, they are a feature of life. More likely to happen in urban areas, than rural; at night rather than by day; to pedestrians rather than car owners; to people walking alone rather than couples or groups. It just so happened that on the way home last night I had to walk by myself through such an area. I don't regard it in terms of "I've been lucky so far" or "My turn had to come." Rather if it's got to happen then please let it happen to me and not to some poor old lady.' He could even look significantly at Hilda when he said 'old lady.'

Yes, he could make it eminently reasonable, uninteresting almost. Was there, though, a danger in this dispassionate approach? Might not the staff think 'He's being too philosophical. He's trying to escape. It's affected him more than he's letting on. Bottling it up. Delayed shock. Better if it all came out.' They'd probably think it their duty to get him emoting – in public. 'You mustn't think we're being inquisitive' – he could hear them saying – 'we want you to get it out your system. That's how people get better. We're only asking for the details for your own good.' Perhaps one of them might even say, though he very much hoped no-one would, 'A jolly good cry can often help'. Being subjected to their solicitation would be worse than a grilling from Hilda.

No, there was nothing for it but to offer a story with just enough realistic detail to ring true. Would Hilda swallow it? She'd often claimed she could tell when someone was lying. 'Some people say the Liar gets shifty or sounds too convincing and confident. Others say the Liar outstares you, dares you to disbelieve. But my way of telling a Liar is different. And it works. And you needn't ask me what it is. I'm not telling.'

That was probably the only thing she didn't tell. He couldn't worry anymore. He was tired of going over all the possibilities. They were getting tedious. He looked at the clock. He had just over three hours to sleep. The morning light would put things in perspective. Maybe his eye would open a bit and he'd see things more clearly.

He turned over, rechecked that he'd set the alarm, determined to get into work before the others. That would give him a territorial advantage.

When he got to work – horribly delayed by the traffic – his colleagues were in the staffroom chatting over their early morning tea, lined up on a row of chairs opposite the lockers, almost waiting for his arrival. There was an awkward silence.

'Whatever happened?'

'Are you alright?'

'You shouldn't have come in.'

'Have some tea.'

He sat down in the only empty chair – and accepted the drink with exaggerated thanks. There was a pause as he sipped it. Hilda Taplin, strangely silent, moved a little in her chair.

'The people who mugged you – for that is what we assume ...' She waited for confirmation. He did not say Yes or No. He breathed deeply, sat on his hands and rocked in order to make himself more malleable when the blow came.

'The people, tell me ...'

She was sitting back, relaxed, the fingers of each hand splayed, the tips touching.

'Tell me ...'

She did not ask as if a question, but as sad confirmation of what she already knew.

'They were ...'

She paused. It seemed an eternity. He knew what she was going to say. His muscles tightened. She smiled at him, indulgent almost.

'They were – weren't they? Blacks?'

He hadn't expected this. He thought she was going to say queer bashers. Immediately she said it he knew he should have foreseen it. He'd thought her predictable to the last phrase, that he knew her inside out! Yet this reaction was so in character, so often her first line of attack. He should've realised she'd be true to her prejudices, that she'd get at him via his opinions, that she'd put point-scoring above seeking the truth.

The implications took time to sink in. All he need say was a simple 'Yes.' He wouldn't have to recite his over-rehearsed speeches. His voice wouldn't have sounded convincing anyway. How could his voice quaver on this one word?

She didn't question the reason for the mugging. It was in Their Nature to do it, to anyone, to themselves. He'd heard her say as much often before. He'd always tried to counter her. But this once, couldn't he just let it pass?

'Oh, come on,' she said. 'I know why you won't reply. You've always stood up for them in the past, haven't you? Now you'll have to admit you were wrong. That I might have been right. Makes a difference when it happens to you, doesn't it?'

Now he didn't even have to say 'Yes.'

'Oh, well,' she said, turning to the other staff. 'That explains everything, doesn't it?'

Adam coughed. He could not let that pass.

'No,' he said. 'No.'

'No?'

'You're wrong.'

'I am?'

It could be so easy. He wasn't going to be a fool and 'confess' now, was he? Enough had been said. He'd be spared more questions. The issue would be closed, no feathers ruffled, all prejudices confirmed and sympathy guaranteed, the whole unwelcome sequence of events soon forgotten, buried in the resumption of trivia and chatter.

What a fool he'd been! All those hours lying awake analysing her character, going over things. Staff reaction! The bar of history. And here she was almost throwing him a lifeline!

'They're not all like that.'

Hilda laughed. 'Who said they were? You'll never learn, will you? Even now. Oh, well. Enough said. Personally I'm not surprised. What do you expect? You never listen properly. I've been saying it for years.'

The familiar old phrases rang out, like a triumphant peal of bells. He didn't mind them now. They'd all been deflected on his behalf.

'There's good and bad in every race,' he said with conviction.

'I've no doubt there is. You don't have to tell me.'

Yes, she had all the certainties. He could almost admire her. She was always there, always would be. He'd been welcomed back into the fold. The prospects were too good to shatter. He couldn't argue. She'd always have the last word anyway. It suited him now to let her.

She got up and walked over. She pulled up his chin.

'Well, let's look at you properly. Doesn't look too bad. No bones broken. It must have been awful, of course. I can just imagine how you felt. You were lucky not to get stabbed. You should've taken a few days off. Then you'd've been spared the buses. I had to wait half an hour this morning. It was too dire for words. Everyone was pushing in. Absolutely no sense of queue at all. You get jostled and pushed. I was lucky not to get knocked over. I can quite see why they put up those notices about pick-pockets. It's almost as bad as being mugged. Believe me. It really IS.'

1, 2, 3, Cock

I DON'T OFTEN COME TO THIS PUB. It's been going for decades, one of the first, and substantially unchanged, resisting juke boxes, piped music, live events and dance, and for that, many thanks. The only refurbishment in forty years involved not more than a day's closure. There was no re-opening ceremony, and none of the regular drinkers could see any difference. The bar assistant, who's worked here for thirty years, a man of few words and expressionless features, merely said, 'It was all a question of the pipework.' The poor soul didn't even register when we pouted our lips and hooted, 'Isn't everything?'

And yet as a quiet venue, a point of reference, for an intimate chat, a reunion to discuss the real changes in the outside world, this pub is without equal.

I'd recently got back into the circuit with a vengeance, after several years of what can most charitably be described as dip, decline and depression. I didn't regard coming here as part of a whirlwind no-stone-unturned tour of the contemporary scene, more as a cosy resting place. I settled down in a quiet, dark empty corner and sipped my drink.

I noticed someone squinting in my direction. I recognised him from long ago. Dreary old bore. I tried to avert my eyes, but too late. He came over.

'Remember me. B? You're A, aren't you? Good God, you're looking young and fit. I hardly recognised you. Mind if I join you?' He looked at my glass. 'You haven't given up drinking, have you? Or found the elixir of life? Tell me the secret. I feel bone tired. I mean bone dry. You must have something to tell. To account for your transformation.'

B had an off-putting in-your-face bonhomie, as well as a supercilious way of having seen, heard and experienced almost everything imaginable. Perhaps I could wind him up, and wind him. If I tell the truth he might take it as a joke, of the sort where the listeners are made to feel uncomfortable, and never sure if they are being got at.

'It's a long story,' I said.

'Got all the time in the world. There aren't many people here, and I noticed they had a delivery this morning, so stocks are high.'

'Well, if you want to hear a story, perhaps you should buy the drinks. Whet my whistle to get me going.'

He obliged and I began.

'It's like this. Give me a piece of paper.' I wrote my name on it, first with my left hand and then with my right. One signature was legible, the other scrawl.

'You can see I'm not ambidextrous. You know the concept of the lead leg, the one you put down first on the flight of stairs, the one that reaches the pavement first. That never applied to me – hands, arms, legs or feet. My brain lobes have always been addled.

'It's no problem, really. I'm lucky. I tend to fit in with custom where it matters. I instinctively hold the knife in my right hand for eating, but when sawing a piece of wood I use the left. I hold the bat on the right side for cricket. I hold a tennis racket with the left. I write, as you can see, with my left, but paint with my right. I do have problems reading maps. I have to position the map in the direction I'm going. I can't re-orientate it in my brain. I can't visualise an architectural ground-plan, work out which room is above another. It's not that I'm in a battle-field of social conditioning versus natural inclination. I have quite marked illogical quirks of co-ordination. I've never been able to switch hands or brain lobes. But I've got by. I made do. You have to. Did you know if you plant a bulb the wrong way round, with the roots uppermost, that the bulb will shuffle, if the earth is loose enough, the right way round? The shoot will always seek the air and light, and the roots will always seek the soil and water. Things have a way … Then a few months ago I sprained my wrist.'

B perceptibly winced. 'I'm sorry to hear that. A really dreadful thing to happen.'

'Well, yes … It was a very novel experience. Most of the things I've ever had wrong with me were not physical, or sporty things, but infections, aches and pains, states of mind, not things localised and verifiable such as a broken bone, but all-over things that needed pills and medicine, that no-one ever knew I was taking. Now it was minor surgery and special exercises. I shared my complaint, rather than creep ashamed to bed. I made my strapped-up wrist a badge of honour. I got people to write their signature on the plaster.'

B looked at my wrists intently. 'Was it the one you

wrote with?'

'No,' I replied. 'It was the one I wanked with.'

A moment's silence, and B snorted. 'I can't imagine you putting up with celibacy. Got someone else to do it for you?'

'Sometimes. But there are occasions when you want peace and quiet, or there's no one round to do it.'

'Much better now, is it?' laughed B. 'Back on the job? Juices still flowing? Higher sperm count than ever?'

'That's not quite the point,' I said irritably. 'The truly marvellous thing is that I broke the habit of a lifetime. I started wanking with my other hand. I dare say most people alternate. But I've always been set in my routines. Then I was forced to change. It wasn't half the same to begin with, then quite suddenly my whole outlook transformed. It was beyond a mere five-minute act. It was as if my brain lobes had suddenly co-ordinated. You can't realise how slow and halting and compensating I once was. I had managed, coped, but never shone, always held back. I wasn't like other boys or able to join in with them. Now I was. I could see things at a glance, a decision was carried out immediately, not put off. I'd always read slowly, at speaking pace. I'd drag my index finger under each word, and hesitate at long words, put off looking up unknown words in the dictionary. Now I can speed read, look at a page of the smallest print and find all the spelling mistakes or typographical errors. Now I can sight-read the most complex music scores. I found I could sing in tune, not only that – I could sing those tongue-twisting patter songs from Rossini and Sullivan. I could read a poem once, and then be able to recite it without the text.

One glance at a set of instructions and the most complex electrical installations became a doddle.

'As for languages – how I used to plod through translations, word by word. I pretended to understand fully what I had only half heard. You're supposed to think in the foreign language – not translate it into English and then translate the reply back into the original language. Now I found I could think in two foreign languages and translate direct from one to the other, by- passing English altogether. I could read a speech from a classic French play and straight away I could hear the speech in naturally-cadenced native Italian.'

'Goodness. All this from wanking with the other hand?'

'Not perhaps in itself. It was a trigger. It pulled a lever. It was as if blockages in my co-ordination had been unplugged or rewired. The power had at last got through. I had ironed out the crumpled sheets, the grey matter in the brain. I was able to achieve all those things I'd so much admired in others. I didn't feel left out, or slobberingly worship rôle models. I had so wanted to be like them, and when I couldn't be I belittled them, claiming that what they were doing wasn't worth the effort. Now I do not question, and surpass them at their own game. Effortlessly. Of course, in a sense, in the act of fitting in I became normal, accepted, indistinguishable from others. This is a loss of identity that I can only retrieve in part by leading a double life, a rich inner imagination, unshared with others, and an outward, healthy social life.'

'Well,' said B, 'Keep your inner life to yourself. No one

will look up to you for that. But for your outward appearance ... you're certainly looking good.' He wouldn't take his eyes off me. 'Slimmer. No flocculence, no cheeks, jowls or tortoise neck. Very good. And all because ... I've heard some things about wanking – makes you this, that, whatever but ... yours isn't exactly a remedy you can patent, is it?'

'It might not work for others. They may not have been in the same needful position.'

B gave me a very strange look. I thought he was going to make some derogatory remark. A minute passed. 'Actually,' he said, 'now we're in confessional mode, something – not really on your level – happened to me. Would you mind ... ?'

'It's not a viagra story, is it? I've heard so many of those. I'm sick of them. Don't let's go down that road.'

'I'll second that,' B said. 'Let me buy you a drink.' He called over to the old barman, 'Same again,' and settled back in his chair. 'One thing you said – really set me thinking. When you sprained your wrist.'

He put his hand on the table. 'Look at that.' He twiddled the thumb, stretched the first finger, the middle finger, the fourth finger. The little finger didn't move. 'You see I've developed ... I can never get the name right – Dupuytren's Contracture. It's not actually the finger, it's at the base. It does straighten, but you have to hold it.' He demonstrated. 'There. You see. Let go and it flops back. It's not locked. It's just that I can't sustain the muscle leverage. A splint would only hold it straight – and staying straight, when the others fingers can bend, would be as bad as being bent when the others are stretched straight. You get what I mean?'

'Yes. I'm sure you're right.'

'I often do wear a splint. It doesn't notice when I wear gloves, which I usually do. I didn't bother me today as I didn't think I was likely to meet anyone I'd need to hide it from in this dreary old dump.'

'It doesn't notice,' I assured him. 'I wouldn't have known if you hadn't pointed it out.' He seemed cheered. 'But I'd know it was there. We're only talking among ourselves. Not as if ...'

'No, indeed.'

I was tempted to ask him – does it actually get in the way when you're doing whatever?'

He continued. 'I've built up a good collection of gloves. Some of them don't look out of place in the summer. They go well with motor-cycle gear. I don't actually have a motor-cycle, but I wear the gear, along the street, and at clubs. No one ever notices. Or says.'

'I expect they're all looking at you in your gear?' I tried to visualise B fully kitted out. It wouldn't surprise me if he wore a size-too-large codpiece.

He went on. 'The splints can be very discreet. A bit of give in them, skin-coloured. And they fit under rubber gloves. Latex. No one has ever said they felt it.

'You mean when you shake hands?'

'No, when I fist their arse.'

'Ouch.'

'They'd actually notice more if I didn't trim my nails.'

'I see. I think.'

'I'm of the opinion that change became inevitable. Not just after my finger went. Looking back, it was something bound to happen. I could have gone down the viagra road, but I've found more pleasure in this. Some of my clients complain when I use the other fist. They say it doesn't feel as good.'

'You can use both hands?'

'And often together, but not both right in.'

He punched the air. He had certainly perked up. Not just the drink, either. His glass was only half empty. I could have done with another one.

'And it's all so reminiscent of old times. Like being in the dark. You don't see clearly – which is what you want in this excessively visual age of ours. Your fantasy is triggered. Under the trees at night you can't make out exactly what you're getting. Even when you get them back home they're looking the other way, face down in the pillow. Well, it's the same in the dungeon. I set up the trestle table and get the client to lie face down. I prop up his crutch with pillows for him to fuck into if he wants. Not that I care what he does. He can imagine whoever he likes is fisting him, and I can get on, and no worries about – what's the word – detumescence. Of course, they don't always look the other way. Not at the place I go now, under the railway arches. It's well-equipped. Stirrups and hammocks. Some like it with a blind-fold. Just put them in position, strap 'em in, and they lay there and take it. Doesn't worry me if I'm not the prime object on their mind. I've got his client ... No, I'll spare you the details.' He paused and went on. 'Some clients insist on paying, even though they're poorer than I am. And then there's this bloke – double our age put together – who insists on the same time every weekday. As I said it's under a railway arch. You can hear the trains slowing down for the station. But come rush hour then the trains for the outer suburbs hurtle through and don't stop. This client always books a slot to catch the train he caught every weekday for thirty years. The six-ten to Chislehurst. The return journey from his work to his wife. The moment the train passes overheard, he shouts "Fuck work. And Fuck you, you old cow. This is what I wanted all the time." '

B burst out laughing at his own narrative. I had to smile.

'I hope you're not developing a violent streak as you grow older.'

'No, I give every consideration, health and hygiene. Won't catch anything bad from this. Takes years of apprenticeship. I'm still a new boy. Learning and observing. Some adopt different angles of approach. Some receive in this club, but give in another. Some give and take, right-hand, left-hand. It's like you and your hands.'

'Is it?'

'Yes. And there's a password in case you get carried away. A password to stop, to get out, not get in.'

'And what may that password be?'

'Hitler.'

'I should have guessed.'

'You'll be surprised how many young men look up to older masters. There is hope for us elderly gays. Not worth going on about the old days, how much better it was cottaging and trolling, or exclusive gentlemen's clubs, and whispered networks. Now there are openings for any age.' He banged down his fist, clenched but for the little finger, and said, 'Regret is not an option.'

'How very butch of you,' I laughed. 'Almost makes me feel better.'

'Yes, and talking of health – fisting is great for rheumatism. Like being buried in sand up to the neck. Never get anything wrong with your wrist.'

'You never sprain it?'

'No, not like you did, doing whatever.'

'I didn't say that's how I sprained it.'

'Come off it. Stands out a mile.'

He was obviously getting carried away, and at my expense. He gave me a violent slap on the back. It was almost certainly time for another drink. It was my round and I called over to the miserable old barman.

In doing so I caught the eyes of a man lounging on a bar-stool. It was C. Oh, God. Him. He was enough to dampen any enthusiasm. He had this reputation of never forging his own links, always trying to get in on the act, hovering round uncertainly when a group gathered. And whenever a couple broke up he was extra-solicitous in the hope of slotting into one or other of the vacancies. He sidled over with an 'Ah!' almost if as we were some after-thought he had suddenly remembered. He asked in an over-familiar gate-crasher voice, 'Mind if I ...' adding not very discreetly, 'Say, you two an item?' When we didn't reply and barely looked up he went on, 'You seem very engrossed.'

We still didn't respond.

'Oh like that, is it?' And with a nervous attempt at being amusing added, 'Deeply. Madly.'

B and I sat back in our chairs and looked at one another.

'We were just confiding. Exchanging stories.'

'Oh, I love a story. Won't tell anyone else. You can trust me with a secret.'

'We can?' B and I said in unison.

'Of, course. You know you can.'

'Do we? Are you sure you could take it? Do you know what you are in for?'

'I can take anything.' He gave a man-of-the-world look.

'We wouldn't want to make you feel uncomfortable. Or anything.'

'Doubt if you'd ever do that,' C said, comfying himself in the chair.

And so B and I repeated the stories we had just exchanged. B told my story – and I might say without missing or exaggerating any incident. I was quite flattered at the attention he must have paid me. And I told B's story, hopefully recalling and illustrating all that he had told me. I felt much better hearing my story coming from someone else's mouth, the first person gaining perspective in becoming the third. And B too seemed far more relaxed. We both looked at C to gauge his reaction.

After a minute or so of nervous silence he said, 'Well, we all have our stories. And they sometimes get exaggerated in the telling.'

'Not these two,' B and I assured him. 'Word for word.'

'Ear to mouth.'

'I see,' replied C.

'And do you have anything to tell us?'

It was an invitation we knew C would find hard to refuse. He took his time replying. We tried to avert our eyes as he nervously shifted in his seat and got into gear.

'I will have. But not on the same level – or how shall I say …?'

'However, you like.'

'It's like this. It hasn't actually happened yet. But it may have to.'

'An implacable inevitability? I sense the Greek over-tones already.'

'It's certainly fraught with dangers.'

'Hanging over you, is it? Sword of Damocles – and all that?'

C paused. 'You've got it. You can tell. I knew I couldn't hide it. You could read what's on my mind. That is uncanny.'

B and I looked at each other.

'I'm for the chop.'

My mind raced. Poor C. We shouldn't have mocked him. Not a death sentence. Fixed time span. Or an op. With 50-50 chance of success?

'You see,' he continued. 'I've got to be circumcised.'

We burst out laughing. 'Is that all?'

'You wouldn't laugh if you knew what I've been through. You can't imagine how I've agonised over it. You're the first I've told. I was always painfully shy. I was even shy in public toilets. Now I lock myself in a cubicle. I thought I'd be able to confide in you. Especially after those stories you told me.'

'Point taken. So…'

'Well,' said C, 'it all began a few months ago …'

Oh, dear I thought. This is going to take ages.

'You can't imagine how red it got.' He wasn't going to take it out and show us, was he? I'm pretty sure I had seen it, at least twenty years ago. I usually remember people more from their members than their faces or characters, but C was such a non-event on all counts that …

'Non-retractable, was the word they used. And phimosis – that's with a ph – and frenulum – that's with an f. I checked them in the medical dictionary and the internet.'

Then he told us at great length all the arguments for and against.

'I'm not boring you, am I? If you've already had it done yourselves then it's not very…'

Neither B not I chose to enlighten him on that topic. It barely seemed relevant.

'Of course,' C continued 'having it done at birth or puberty … it's less dangerous and you rarely hear of anything going wrong. But at my age …'

'Surely it's not an age thing, is it?' B asked.

'No, but …'

'Oh, come off it. It's only a local anaesthetic.'

'But the cut, the cauterising, and what was the other thing? The suture incision …'

'Just words.'

'There have been fatalities. Permanent issues of blood, life-threatening infections, too much cut off, partial amputation of the … You don't understand … But no, I'm not worried about the op itself. It's the …'

'Psycho drama,' I put in heartlessly. 'You secretly love it. Calm down. Look at it like this.' And I put on my counselling hat, and voice. 'It's not many people your age who have the chance to make radical decisions about their life 'downstairs'. For most people our age it's already a closed book. Memories, and not much else. It needn't be so. You heard how I rejuvenated, and how B has compensated. We only met at this dried-up old watering hole by chance. On reflection it might have been Fate. We've both benefitted from exchanging stories, and now we're in a position to help you. Difficult decisions have to be made. Manfully. Go ahead with this operation. You'll get full medical after-care, and when the situation's settled down, and you've made the necessary intimate and private tests, come and tell us all your impressions. It's a before-and-after moment for you. With possibilities of a daily diary entry. Which even if never published you can draw on in conversation. And what a fascinating topic you've chosen! We'll certainly be happy to tune in, and who knows your experience may well prove a form of counselling for others – even possibly ourselves – should we find ourselves in a similar position.'

'Oh, thank you,' cried C. 'That is *so* reassuring.' He gave me a look as if I were a wise elder brother. 'I did think fleetingly you mightn't want to know. But the thought of being able to share my intimate experiences with both of you – at some future time – will surely keep me going through – the undoubtedly difficult times ahead.'

'What a mature attitude on your part! You will be in our thoughts – and would, were we religious, be in our prayers.'

'And you'll be able to stand proud in public toilets.'

We patted him on the knee. And called over to the bar for a round of drinks.

Our conversation became more relaxed. We discussed the usual topics about getting old. B said the more he lost his cranial hair, the more it compensated further down in his ears, nostrils and eyebrows.

'And even downstairs it's kept its colour, and mocks everything around it.'

'Don't let that stop you,' I said. 'There's still a range of possibilities. Change of position. Turn bisexual …'

'Go on the game even,' said B. 'There have always been some youngsters who like older men. I recently heard of this young millionaire who wanted to look after an old tramp.'

'Really,' I said. 'Hate yuppies and City Slickers though I undoubtedly do, if I was offered a bargain like that I might well accept.'

We both laughed. B told another story. This time about his aged friend D, whose right bollock suddenly began to hang lower than the left. 'You can imagine the effect this had on his behaviour patterns,' laughed B. C joined in with a story and told that he had recently read a crime thriller in which a maiden aunt murdered her rich yuppie nephew.

'That's where the money is,' we all agreed. 'Exploit the young. They did it enough to us.'

'I still miss some of the old ways,' lamented B. 'They got you out of doors. Trolling and cottaging.' He said he dreamt about setting up a chain of mobile toilets, a kind of pre-fab on the back of a trailer. 'It goes on a circuit between trolling areas, you hail and ride, hop-on hop-off. I thought we could charge a penny in old money. I've still got a bagful at home.'

After a pause C said, 'And there's always viagra.'

'No. Please. I've heard so many of those stories. A moratorium please. This is a serious get-together.'

C looked cowed, but agreed amicably enough. I felt guilty at having mocked him. Yet in our jovial mood I did feel the need of …

The barman shuffled over. At the same pace he had always moved, with the same expressionless face and probably the same limited vocabulary. If we wanted a target surely he was fair game. Get-at-able. A nice prod to round off the evening.

'Last orders.' He began clearing up the glasses.

'Can we ask you something?' He barely looked up and continued collecting the glasses. 'I know you've worked here for thirty years, but did you realise this was designated a gay pub?'

He looked at us without blinking.

'Yes. I had been informed. Sometime ago I believe.'

His voice was flat and lifeless, and his face as unfazed as a dead haddock. I longed to make it register in some way.

'Tell me. Have you ever been to bed with a woman?'

He remained unflappable, and continued working almost as if he hadn't heard. The glasses on his laden tray did not rattle or betray him. In his own good time he turned his back on us and shuffled towards the bar. Half-way there he let out a tremendous fart.

Tagged

QUESTION TAGS ARE POINTLESS?
Aren't they?

They don't expect an answer. And rarely prompt a reply. These days few people use them. Except the all-encompassing Isn't it? Or more likely Innit?

Sad. I contend there's a loss of nuance.

The negative tag can become a positive injunction.

'Be a good boy, won't you?'

A positive tag can reveal a negative attitude.

'You won't be a bad boy, will you?'

Both examples mean the same.

'You will be on time, won't you?' This is almost trusting, as if the person spoken to has already given an assurance.

'You won't be late, will you?' This casts doubt, and dares the listener to defy the speaker.

Of course the tone of voice and inflexion count as well, as can the social position, family relationship, and age difference between the speaker and the spoken to.

I was reminded of this by a woman, whom I keep bumping into. I seem to bump into her the more I try to avoid her. She's obviously unable to blend into the background, or play mollusc and attach to a rock. Her clothes are 'foreign' in the sense of yesteryear. Long dress, long floppy sleeves, high collar. No wrist or ankle exposed, and yet somehow revealing more about her than if she were half-clad.

She is startlingly direct when she speaks. She always addresses her comments or commands to you – you being the world, a stranger, an inanimate object – and always rounds them off with the same question tag. I'm not sure if the written version would end with a question mark or an exclamation mark. It is more in the nature of an order.

'Get out of my way, will you?' This is usually addressed to pedestrians or people in front of her in a queue. She also says it to cars as she strides across a busy road without looking where she's going.

'Come here, will you?' is her most frequent mode of attracting attention at reception desks and shop counters, or as she extracts a small coin from her purse.

'Get in there, will you?' This is mainly reserved for inanimate objects, such as when she is stuffing valueless items into her voluminous carrier bags.

Other variants are used as necessary. For instance, if she's sitting on a park bench and a dog approaches 'Go and crap somewhere else, will you.' The tone throughout is of an exasperated mother not up to it, as if she has an imaginary child who cannot be trusted, and is in continual need of correction.

Oh well, there but for the … etc. She both revolts and fascinates. One day I stood looking at her for perhaps that second too long, risking eye contact and another typical response 'Fuck off, will you?'

In fact, I was not the only person watching her. A man standing near me asked –

'You know who she is, don't you?'

I smiled. Actually, I didn't know who he thought he was, standing so close and talking to me uninvited. He must have been watching me as I was looking at her.

'You know who she is. Don't you?' he repeated

I wondered why he supposed I should know her. Was she some celebrity fallen from grace?

'She's your mother.'

Now that was an extremely interesting proposition. And not all that preposterous. I hadn't seen my mother since we fell out, years ago. Nor indeed any of my family. So, from that angle – for all I knew – she might have been my mother. Before I could ask the man 'Why should you think that?' he had disappeared. I was left to answer the question he had posed.

In all probability it was her. There were the inevitable similarities and parallels you can barrel-scrape to prove any theory. The clinching evidence was that dreadful use of question tags.

When I was a child Mother never failed to warn me, threaten me, and call me to heel, always couching her commands in the same semi-question form. 'Be quiet, will you?' 'Come here, will you.' 'Don't do that, will you?' 'Listen to me, will you.' 'Don't put your finger in your ear, will you.' She said it almost implying 'wilful.' It was unrelenting, and from a very early age.

The reverse word order of the subject and the verb should really have determined the meaning. 'You will do this' is an order. 'Will you do this?' is a request and partial question. She went one further, by putting the 'will you' at the end of the sentence. And though it is not a question in the exact definition of the word she made it one by pronouncing it as if it had an aitch. Whill you. Most of the WH question words – Why? When? Where? Which? What? – have a distinct Whoosh to start them off. This led to a misunderstanding that was to change my life.

The few people who ever came into contact with Mother often took her to be slightly foreign. She never chose to speak to them. They only knew her from over-hearing the orders she barked at me. 'Come back here, will you.' 'Don't go over there, will you?' 'Keep away from those people, will you.'

The neighbours mistook the question tag, and took it to be my name. Not 'Come here, will you?' but 'Come here, Will-Hugh.' Some corruption of William and Hubert. Or Wilfred and Hugh. Possibly a foreign version, Wilhui – or Wilheu – which looked slightly Flemish or Dutch.

The neighbours took pity on me and on the rare occasions I was alone would approach and say 'Hello, Will-Hugh, you're looking well.' 'Tell me, Will-Hew, what have you been doing today?' I found their cretinous grins and coo-ing baby tones hardly less sufferable than Mother's continual prohibitions.

The saving grace was that if they could take the question tag to be my name, why shouldn't I? I quite liked the name. It was a new identity and set me off on new paths. It was not the name my parents had chosen for me, and which appeared on my birth certificate. Mother rarely addressed me directly, and never chose to use my official first name. My surname was different to my mother's. I took it to be my father's. It was almost as if I was from a totally different family. I had no qualms about thinking of myself as the problematical question tag. And later when I began to move in circles that would have shocked my mother I adopted the name. And ensured I was only ever known by that name. I gave it out to my associates in the criminal world. And it came very useful when I began dating men.

'What's your name?' a pick-up would ask.

'Will-Hew.'

'That's a strange name. How do you spell it?'

'Good question,' I'd say non-committally.

'Foreign?'

'Half so. Not from these parts.'

'Real name, or sobriquet?'

'What my mother always called me.'

'I see. An internal family name? A pet name? Only used by close relatives?'

It was as if I had invited them into the inner circle of a tight-knit family. How flattered they were! How they told me secrets about themselves, more perhaps than they would ever have done had they known the path along which I was to develop. It certainly got me more men than if I'd adopted one of those silly names that were so fashionable in all-male circles, feminine diminutives, ranks of royalty, or a take-offs of a media person.

I tested the name in distant pick-up places. Everybody

fell for it. They had never bumped into anyone else with the same name. And they never knew how to spell it, so that their evidence, their reliability as a witness, was discountenanced from the start by the police, who had no record of anyone of that name. Truly, nomenclature is destiny.

It certainly proved so when I went to Antwerp, or Anvers if you like, the undoubted centre of the diamond trade, and where I was to make my mark. There my name sounded right. Most of the traders were non-residents – English-speakers valiantly trying to speak another language. They took me to be local, and to have local knowledge, and underground contacts. They used me as their intermediary.

'Will you go to the bank? Will you do a job for us?' Questions these may have been, but I took the Will you to be a mispronunciation of Will-Heu. I was being singled out and given an order. I obeyed, and next time volunteered. Promotion came quickly. And the little outfit I had set up on the side soon outwitted much larger rivals. It was the name that did it. No doubt about it. Mother had given me a head-start in a way she could never have intended.

Yet I could never thank her, or laugh off the reversal of intent. The reason for our falling-out was always in the back of my mind. When I was a young child her bossiness could be construed as indicating some concern for my welfare. But her tone and tack changed when I grew older and larger. 'Don't fall in the water, will you' became 'You won't fall in the water, will you?' Oh, the potential between the 'Don't' and 'Won't'! I was now given an option. And in a derisive tone. 'Mind you don't fall in the water.' As if I couldn't work out for myself it would be a silly thing to do. She thought it was the just the sort of thing I would do. Something she'd secretly like me to do! 'Mind you don't' had become 'Why don't you?' She would have relished my defying her. Just to prove her point. She was tempting me in a direction, to my own public humiliation, and destruction. The over-protective advice had become the belittling put-down. She had transformed from an over-powering mother, towering over me, to a troll, implanting doubts, in the faintest taunting voice, and not even necessarily in my presence.

'Mind you don't slip on the ice.' And when I did, I would feel the laughter shaking in her hands as she helped me up.

Ah, there she is, poor dear. Fallen on her own hard times. Far from an object for amusement. Perhaps realising, but not yet letting go. Not yet for her a nodding-head and the Acceptance World. But alone and cursing anyone who gets too close, even to her own shadow. She's not yet got what they call the Forgetful. But in view of all I've done can I expect her, would I want her, to recognise and acknowledge me?

She still gives the impression of being in control, going somewhere, and in a hurry. She might turn a corner, stop, and go back the same way. Not always, not predictably, not reduced to the stereotype of say, the drunk who swings round the lamp-post and goes the way he came.

One day, she chose to wait at a pedestrian crossing and

not barge straight into the traffic. Next to her was a jogger, barely out of her teens, half-clad, running on the spot, going no-where until the lights changed, when she sped off, limbs propelling her forward, only her pony tail swinging to a contrary pendulum. And my mother, given the opportunity of crossing, hesitated, blamed the traffic for resuming its juggernaut.

While watching this I noticed out the corner of my eye that same man watching her. He seemed to be stalking the poor woman. That was up to him, and not for me to intervene. But had he been watching me as well?

He turned and smiled. 'And do you know who I am?'

He looked younger than before. He was quite good looking. Years ago perhaps I might have said Yes to his advances.

'And do you know who I am?' he repeated.

I'm pretty sure I'd never seen him before – or known him carnally.

'I'm your brother.'

O My Good Godness

I WAS EXHAUSTED AND RUDDERLESS, as after having achieved a major and significant goal. I knew I could only restore my spirits by undertaking yet another meaningful and worthwhile task. I didn't know exactly what, but I knew it would be on the same general topic, and involving similar research techniques as the goal I had recently completed.

That task had taken me over three years, and had involved visiting innumerable art galleries in Northern Europe. As an art historian I am meticulous in the gathering of material, insisting I see all I comment on, and relegating unseen material to an appendix. I approach each painting from every possible angle, date, attribution, the life of the artist and his contemporaries, the local traditions and the materials available, the identification of the sitter, the subject of the picture, and how it has been treated by other artists, and the subsequent history of the painting and its owners, and very often of the frame. All this is minutely chronicled, and illustrated with photos, exactly reproducing the colours in the painting, and the photos are correctly aligned with the text to form a complete and authoritative monograph. I use the word monograph, for this need not imply a work on a single artist, but on a theme, often rarefied, and in my case unique.

I am not prepared to repeat other people's work, or just add a gloss to existing knowledge, some minor reinterpretation, or a mere dust-down of a neglected artist for a routine periodic revaluation. I might be persuaded to deal with an undiscovered artist whom I felt justified exhaustive research, but only in the knowledge that my work on him would for all time remain the definitive one.

As it was, I had to select a smaller but significant side-line that itself would illumine the whole work. Not perhaps the central figures, the infinite variations possible of a standard religious grouping, or the differing ways different ages and artists had approached the same myth. More perhaps the peripheral extras and also-rans, the hidden detail that only an intimate study can highlight, and which can often prove as revealing to the life-style of the period as to the mind of the artist. I always identify with the off-centres, the daily goings-on unruffled by the high drama. The position of handmaidens has always fascinated me, and the manservant: the attendant spirits, as it were. And also, of course, of animals.

Much has been written of animals in art, of specific animals, the dog in particular, as the loyal defender of the master huntsman. Much mention has been made, though incidental and never in a separate monograph, on displays of affection between dogs, mating dogs, tucked away in the corners, filling a gap in the painting, but in reality, illuminating the whole canvas, appearing on the surface as a 'nice touch', a homely addition, on a lower level than the main canvas, but which paint analysis and x-rays have shown were always an integral part of the picture, and often the very starting point for the whole composition. I was determined to upgrade these forgotten and peripheral subjects, and with all this in mind, and after a thorough search to make sure I was not duplicating anyone else's work, or work in progress, I honed in on my chosen theme, shitting dogs in art.

I knew from the outset that the Netherlands – note the Nether – would be my centre of operations. Dutch artists especially in the seventeenth century loved homely scenes, scenes of low life, set in bawdy taverns, with loosened collars, splayed legs, and suggestive clay pipes. Dogs were always in tow. While the master got drunk the dogs went about their business. The Dutch have always had a penchant for lavatory humour. Certainly, their present-day toilet design encourages this belief. It is not a U-bend. The excreta falls on a porcelain tray. The smell and sight lingers. It may be easier to flush away, even handier to clean than the conventional U-bend, but is less discreet.

And the Dutch language, never beautiful, is much given to sounds of eructation. I never forget being on a train coming into the terminus of The Hague. The conductor called out the name of the approaching station. Den Haag. Den Haag. He made the double A so elongated it sounded like a bowel strain after a four-egg omelette.

Similarly Dutch notices against dog-fouling show a dog, with its tail upheld, and above the goodly pile of excrement are wisps to suggest it is still hot and steaming. Such details may seem unnecessary, but I would opine come from a long and honourable tradition of portraying dogs at stool.

Certainly, the number of such instances in Dutch Art is quite remarkable. I had no idea my research would take so long or involve visiting so many small and out-of-the-way galleries and private collections. Or that so many different varieties of dog breed would be included. Everyone knows of the elegant whippet, back arched like a croquet hoop, feet in a bunch, tail over its back, eyes focused on the middle distance, almost poised on the touch line, ready to leap forwards, a quick kick backwards, and a race out of sight. But there are many other breeds, more docile home dogs, miniatures, some unidentifiable, and the oddest crossbreeds. So many indeed, that they piled up and up to form a monograph of several hundred pages. I took the manuscript to the finest of printers, where I ordered a print run of fifty copies, all of which I signed. It is an esoteric subject, and I never expect sales to be great. There are some minor changes I would make were there ever to be a second edition, but I am for the most part satisfied with a worthwhile job well done.

But how to follow it up? Something totally different was called for. And please let it be in more clement climes. I had enough of bending double with a torch and magnifying glass peering into the bottom corners of dark pictures in freezing, out-of-the way galleries. The warm South beckoned. Any facet of Italian art would be congenial, some topic inexplicably avoided, but which if gathered together under one heading would form the basis of a pioneering monograph, and lay the foundation stone for future studies. Again, it was to the peripheral that I gravitated. Not the dogs in the bottom corners, but higher up and airborne the angels, putti, and cupid figures. Like secular, anthropomorphic halos, they hovered in unlikely positions, around the central figures, their tubby limbs tucked behind to show a dimpled knee. How small their wings were! Barely large or feathered enough to buoy them up. And how small their genitals! Had anyone I wondered ever written a monograph on the comparative presentation in art and sculpture of the genitalia of angels? Or come to that of cupids, putti, fauns and dryads? My copious searches found no scholar had hit upon the potential significance of such a work. I was more than happy it be my own. No competition. No forbears. Plain sailing. A subject that would undoubtedly add significant knowledge to the History of Art.

I set out full of confidence, humbled only by the immensity of the task, encouraged by the certain knowledge of the plaudits it would win. If the Dog monograph had not sold then the new project most surely would.

The major galleries proved no problem. I flicked through the catalogues of their permanent collections, double-checked the latest acquisitions, and honed in on any likely paintings. Most were to be found in the reserve collections, to which I needed to apply for entry, and where I was free to pursue my research without interruption. It became obvious which types of painting and periods I should aim for. I dispensed with ninety percent of portraits and historical paintings, and concentrated on the religious and the mythological. As to individual topics, popular through many centuries, the haul was varied.

There was nothing of relevance in the many versions of the ever-popular topic, The Rape of the Sabines. And surprisingly The Massacre of the Innocents proved disappointing. It was full of babies being torn from their mother's arms but never once was there a portrayal of clothing being pulled off far enough to reveal the vitals. Even the dead babies scattered on the foreground were depicted with the genitalia discreetly covered. Likewise, it was obvious from the various depictions of The Origin of the Milky Way that a spurting breast did not do much for the attendant naked putti.

As to individual artists, I was saddened that the repressed soul of Carlo Crivelli, who gave such full and hairy nipples to the most scraggy and asthenic of martyrs, insisted on swathing his airborne putti in the most cumbersome clothing. Far more interesting was Cima di Conegliano. He obviously bothered about the genitalia of his Christ Childs and angels and gave them perky, three-dimensional, though at this tender age not tripartite, members, rather resembling a short-handled lavatory plunger, which, if nothing else, certainly made a change from the perfunctory little whelks most artists portrayed. Many artists appeared to be under the edict of shame that led the wretched Daniel da Volterra to paint the cover-ups in the Sistine Chapel.

There was much to research, and I widened my remit as well as my consciousness. I have no great love for the founders of religions, nor the father figures, prophets and intercessors, not even the angels and heavenly messengers, but I loved the attendant spirits, the putti, the nymphs and dryads. They were beyond the morality attached to mere religion. They cock a snook, and innocently and unashamedly show off their underdeveloped hairless crutch, almost as an antidote to the hairy-thighed fauns and herms – not that I was averse to giving them a second glance!

Naturally much of my work was necessarily public, especially the camera shots, and this attracted the attention of bystanders. It was essential that each shot was exactly to scale, but even with sophisticated modern cameras I occasionally needed to take measurements. There are several discreet ways of doing this, but only one for outside statues in the blazing sun, and that is a ladder and tape measure. This caused much giggling among the crowds of little children. They were very understanding when I explained my project in detail to them, even more so when I threw some coins in their direction.

Less happy was a young man, whom I had noticed following me round. I took him to be an erstwhile student, and thought perhaps that he had mistaken me for an established artist, or moulder of opinions. Just as I was about to take him into my confidence he rounded on me with the words 'You're the man who groped my baby brother!'

It was at least two weeks before both my black eyes were open enough for me to continue my research. I became wary that my work might be under surveillance, and for that reason I kept my ever-growing file with me at all times. I also worried about the safety of the camera and arranged for 'hard copies' of the photos to be printed out at the end of each day. I realised that there could be chemists, who though dedicated to the scientific

approach, might sometimes be weighed down by consid-
erations of a moral nature, or even a hatred of art. I
assured the chemists in question that the photos were not
of living genitalia, but part of a comparative art-historical
project. They did not seem convinced at first, but after
paying almost ten times the normal rate for developing
the photos they reluctantly acquiesced.

I was growing so apprehensive and edgy that I recoiled
sharply when a middle-aged cleric put his hand on my
shoulder. He smiled and said he had been following me
for some time, and how much he appreciated the work I
was doing. I had never thought to meet a fellow
appreciator, someone to encourage my work, and from
the start I suspected he was a rival researcher, come to
steal my findings.

'Ah, what it is to be able to share one's joy in such
things. You know,' he said, pointing to a faun's member,
'this is what brought me into the Church. All those years
ago! My job is high up now and administrative, but I
never fail to pop into galleries. There was a lovely little
Eros in Room 5. Impish and … what's the word? You
know how it is? Have you thought how odd it is that
Eros, the bringer of love, never gets aroused himself? But
not perhaps odd on reflection. What, after all, does the
matchmaker get from making the match?'

I did not reply. The man unnerved me. I moved away,
and said, 'Room 5, you say?'

'Not any more, luv. It's being restored. Lucky the
restorer who gets down on Eros! Might find the artist's
original intentions were far more ambitious, eh?'

I shuddered. What was I being taken for? Some form

of pervert?

The cleric continued. 'Little Imps, aren't they? Bet they get up to some antics among themselves when the lights are out. Dimpled grin, knees and . . . sinister as well as cute. You can't really call them cocks, can you? That's too adult a word for those twinkled, wrinkled, fascinatingly innocent and . . .' He tailed off. 'Probably never be used for their real purpose, of course. Certainly not in the case of angels. Just tinkles from a height for them. Ah, but the fauns? They're the ones you should go for!'

I could listen to no more, and made my exit. The man was a nonce and abuser, even if not practising. What was the point of sex with children? You'd have to tell them what to do, and they'd have nothing to do it with! Wait another ten or fifteen years and I could well see some purpose.

Once I had researched all the Galleries as far south as Naples I braced myself for the Deep South. It was less charted, but offered challenges and prospects. Baroque lasted here for many centuries, and in some areas paralleled residual pagan influences.

I spent months going from small town to town, travelling with more and more equipment, checking every church, picture and local artist. I began to feel the input vastly exceeded the outcome. In some of the more remote and inhospitable towns I discovered the evil eye was still a much-held belief. I did not want to give the wrong impression, and spoke the least and tipped all what I could afford.

One morning when the sun was high and I was just

about to enter a church to view a picture I had high hopes for, I felt a hand on my shoulder. Oh no! Not another bloody tormentor, come to interrupt my work and mistake my motives! In fact, a young man, rather fetching and very apologetic. He smiled at me and nodded welcome.

'I understand your research. I have been watching you. It is good. Unusual. I have no problem. You are an artist and writer. It is different for them. You see things from another angle. It is good.'

I have to admit I was flattered.

'Here, you will find your biggest test. You come to our town, small as towns go. You cannot leave without a visit to somewhere very special. I can offer you more than you have come across so far.'

I was suspicious, but let him continue.

'Let me explain. This is the time of the Transumanza, when the herdsmen bring their flocks down from the hills for pasture. Goatherds, shepherds, even cowherds and some swineherds. It is seasonal. It has happened since way back. Before Christ. Before God. You have seen this before?'

I shook my head. He pointed out of town to a river valley.

'You arrive too late to see the seasonal river in flood with the melt-water. Now you see it dry and strewn with stones brought down by the flood. Look closer. There are isolated pools, in the deeper sides of a river bend, or caught under the piers of bridges. There, the seeds, both air and water-borne, take root and fringe each little watering hole and became the centre of attention for the herds. You have seen such things? No? You will come to find the seasonal nature of things most endearing.'

'Yes?'

'You have come at the right time. Something brought you here, though you do not know it. You will not be disappointed. It will be a great time, as well, for the herdsmen. They can relax. They know their herds will not go without, or wander far, but just follow the riverbed. The herdsmen are then free to enjoy themselves. You have seen them close up?'

'No.'

'They are like fauns, bronzed and hairy, and smell of the animals they tend. You should see them milk their flock, their large hands squeezing the long suggestive teats. They are the fauns, come down once a year,' and he added, laughing, 'almost like at Easter time!'

I looked at him. He was a handsome brute, his stubble catching the sun and glinting. But what was he really telling me? What was he taking me for?

He smiled, a very knowing smile. 'It is a good time for the women as well. The childless women. Infertility, miscarriages, still-birth, infant mortality. They all go down to the riverbank at night, and give themselves to the herdsmen. Then the river flows again. The river of life!'

'Good Lord,' I exclaimed. 'I've never heard of this before. I've never seen it represented in Art.'

'No, you wouldn't have done. But it is a fact, even if not verified in Art. Those that need to – they give themselves to the shepherds, the goatherds, the swineherds, the cowherds. It means nothing to these herdsmen. Many of them are orphans, unwanted at birth and exposed on the hillsides. They survived and now descend to repopulate. It is a continuum. It is a matter of indifference to them who ...' he paused, 'or should I say whom? – they fuck. Or indeed what they fuck. They are like animals, and have a season for such things.'

'Great God! And do the women get pregnant?'

'Always. The husbands will accept the babies as their own. No questions will be asked. Thus, was it ever, and ever shall be.'

'GesuMaria. But why are you telling me this?'

'I know you to be a serious scholar. These ancient customs cannot interest you. Surprise you, yes. What will be of interest to you is this.'

'Yes?'

'Before the women can go down to the river bank they must first obtain absolution. It is the only intervention the Church makes, the only acknowledgement the Church gives to these customs.'

He pointed half way up the hillside. 'See those caves. They are empty now, and are sometimes used in winter by the herdsmen. Once they were troglodyte dwellings, a remote community. But,' he laughed, 'nothing, as we know, is out of the orbit of Mother Church. One of the caves is a church, a crypt almost. It contains a miracle-working painting. It is displayed only once a year. For half an hour. It is locally known – and forgive the locals for having no appreciation of Art – as The Cupid of the Long Cock.'

'Now that would really be a coup for my monograph. I must see it. Take me there.'

'I thought you might say that. It is not that easy.

Remember a half an hour a year.'

'No time at all to study an unknown work.'

'There can be no photography.'

'I can survive that.'

'Let me tell you more, before you get carried away. The childless women gather there, approaching the steep incline on their knees, some pushing heavy stones in front of them. Are you marking me well? If you were not a scholar, given to genuine research, I would tell you nothing of this.'

'Get on with it. Tell me what I must do.'

'It will be necessary for you to go as a woman. Against the grain you are about to tell me, but for the sake of your art you will do anything? Have I read your mind?' He laughed. 'You must also bring money. Above all, remember it is a matter of the utmost seriousness to these women. Do not let them discover you. They would act like harpies out for revenge if they knew you had been in on their secret. I would suggest you blend in. Knitted socks, a long skirt, shawl and head scarf. Pretend you're deaf and dumb, and from a neighbouring village. Can you do this?'

'Is there no other way?'

'There is, but it would be more difficult.'

'Let me judge that.'

'If you wanted a personal audience, to look at the painting for ten minutes, charged at exorbitant rates, then you must book several months ahead. The procedure is this. Come on your birthday, with your birth certificate. You can only see the painting exactly nine months to the day before your birthday. That was when your father's penis was at its biggest and most productive, and proven to be used for reproduction and not pleasure. This is the necessary proviso the Church makes. Again, you would have to go as a woman, and this time you would be thoroughly questioned and stripped.'

'That is obviously out of the question,' I conceded.

'Then you must go on your knees.'

I could not but agree to this arrangement, and counted the days and hours till it was due.

Great stones had fallen on the steps and path to the cave church. Just as the melt-waters had brought stones to the riverbed, so some landslide or other had lodged the boulders here. They blocked all progress, and the women, one after another, crawled to the front to try to move them. When my turn came, I managed to roll the largest boulders downhill, safely out of the way of the women assembled below. For this I got a cheer and established a position near the front.

It became decidedly breezy the higher we got and only after a time could I distinguish the sigh of the wind from the sound of a flute, then of a tambour and antic cymbal. Three herdsmen, squatting cross-legged on a ledge, played a mocking serenade as we passed. I could not be sure, but I think one of them was my mentor. I was certainly given a knowing grin and shrug as if to say 'If you have faith, who knows where that faith will lead? All is possible in the domain of Eros.'

We squeezed into the cave church. It was windowless like a crypt, but large enough to accommodate the fifty or so women who had made the ascent. The sole door was closed behind us. An androgynous looking functionary lit candles and pulled a drape off the far wall to reveal a painting of some form. It took time to adjust one's eyes, and I couldn't make out if it were a mural or a framed painting. The work certainly needed a clean, and had not benefited from storage in the damp cave or exposure to the smoke and heat of candles. The edges and background were almost blanked out. Only the two main figures were reasonably clear.

A woman lay back receptive, propped on cushions. One arm, behind her neck, high-lit a perfectly-formed breast. The other breast was obscured by a cascade of long curly hair. Her outstretched legs led the eye inexorably to a mound of golden ringlets. She was the Goddess Abundance swathed in a robe whose crinkles and flat surfaces ranged in colour from sky-blue and sea-blue to the dark grey of angry clouds.

The Eros figure, though muscular, handsome and with a winning smile, had wings barely large enough to get him airborne, let alone to perform aerobatics, on his headlong, unstoppable trajectory towards the woman. Just as disproportionate was the enormous quiver, suggestively low-slung about his thighs.

It was at most the work of a local artist, provincial in the extreme. The suggestiveness could well have been by default, the sheer inability of the artist to appreciate relative human proportions. Alternatively, it might have been the intentional and wilful work of a new and untutored apprentice, making merry at his master's expense. If so, the joke had backfired, and the picture was now taken in earnest, and the work of the master of the studio forgotten. It was even possible that the scurrilous work was painted on the reverse of a more serious canvas, and the wrong side was framed, so that the true work of art still remains unseen.

Be that as it may, one had, grudgingly to admit it was, even in its imperfections, an arresting image. Truly, nowhere in my copious researches had I seen an Eros or putti, least of all an angel, so well-endowed and so determined to put his assets to such good use. Another second and he would, by gravity or intent, alight on the woman, and be on her and up her, with her outstretched arm around him pulling tighter. I blinked and expected to open my eyes to a scene of full copulation, limbs inextricably linked and ecstatic eyes cast heavenwards. But the picture had stayed the same.

Or had it? With my experienced art-critic's eye I began to note details that might escape less seasoned viewers. The women cramped in the cave were muttering imprecations, nodding, crying, or playing worry beads with the money they were going to donate. I did not like to ask them to move over so I could check the details more closely. Nonetheless, even from a distance and an awkward sightline … Yes, by God! The figures were changing imperceptibly, and as if self-conscious, had partially re-clothed. A halo now lodged in the hair above the woman's head, and her robe was the uniform unvaried dark blue associated with the Virgin. Round Eros's neck was a crucifix, and the centre of his palms were punctured. And what I had taken for sweat, now appeared as blood. But the quiver had grown unmistakably phallic and massively distended. The picture was now little short of the ultimate sacrilege. Virgin and Christ – that pure relationship of mother and son – had been redefined and sullied forever! Our Lord as mother-fucker.

This implication seemed to escape the swaying mass of praying women. They were in a trance, oblivious to the world, getting distinctly overheated and giving off body odours I could well have done without. There was no way I could extricate myself. The atmosphere bore down on my chest. I could hardly contain my outrage and was relieved when the half-hour was up and the candles were extinguished. The women dropped the coins into the collection box, trouped out the cave, and filed singly down the hillside.

I stood alone at the cave entrance, glad of the certainly of light and fresh air.

That it should come to this! Or a life of penance in one of the caves?

There was only one thing to do. I renounced my life's work, easily done, as no-one knew of it. I tore off my woman's clothing, trampled on the wig, smudged the slap off my face with spit. Then, restored to manhood, I unzipped my folder, which had grown so large with my researches, and pulled out a wodge of papers and scattered them to the breeze. As I did so the breeze gathered force and lifted the papers, and all the subsequent handfuls, chapters, notes and appendices, and lifted them, still grouped in chapters as if herded together, further and further up the hillside until they were all lost to sight in the snow caps.

I bounded downhill, without a thought for my safety, nimble-footed as a gazelle. I soon overtook the women and was first at the riverbank for a man-size bite at a goatherd's cock.

Vicarious

HE WAS THE ONLY THING GOING at the time. He'd been hovering round the entrance to the toilets for over an hour, making pleasantries to anyone who hadn't struck lucky. I could only assume he was rent. I offered him the going rate, and we went back to my place. Nothing happened.

As he was dressing he asked if he could see me again.

'What's the point?' I thought. I'm not made of money, and don't take kindly to time-wasters and cock-teasers. He smiled. Really quite engagingly. And in an odd way I felt I'd been adopted.

A week later Omar – that was the name he gave – came round with a young man, very similar to him, in age and build. I made coffee for them both, and then Omar got up and said, 'I have to go.' I didn't try to stop him. The young man and I enjoyed a steamy night, so memorable and so unrepeatable that I hoped I'd never see him again.

Omar phoned later that week. He didn't ask for money or enquire what had happened. He just said, 'I think I know your tastes. I'll keep looking for you.' When he phoned again his first words were, 'I have someone for you.' It was all so unexpected and welcome I didn't stop to wonder what Omar's motivation might be.

He clarified the situation on his next visit. He asked if he could watch us at it. 'Let me stay, please. Don't make me go.' If I refused he might not bring anyone else round. The young man he'd brought didn't seem to mind.

Omar stood behind us at the end of the bed. I was self-conscious at first, but once you get beyond a certain stage auto-pilot takes over and you don't stop until both tanks have been emptied. When it was over I was surprised to find Omar gone. He had made no noise, and left no tell-tale signs.

I tried to relate all this to similar occurrences. There was this man, a regular over the Common, who always stood by groups and couples. He never got too close or joined in, but his presence was irritating. We called him The Looker. On more than one occasion he was challenged and driven away. He would always give a howl of epileptic proportions, as if he was being dragged from the thing dearest to him and led off to execution.

And then there was Hadley, who always used to winter in North Africa, but found the situation there increasingly problematical. He now held open house, and befriended any foreign like-minds whose government or religion forced them into a double life or exile. He threw regular parties, paired off his guests, and allowed access to his several spare bedrooms. He never did anything with anyone, but gained the greatest satisfaction from match-making.

I suppose it was irrelevant to the man on the Common exactly whom he was looking at, and to Hadley whom he was pairing off. But as far as I knew Omar was not a looker or matchmaker. He seemed to have latched onto me exclusively. Which in a way was quite flattering. I can't imagine what he gained by just looking, or what in particular he saw in me. But almost every night he brought someone new around.

And the odd thing was I began to notice the person he brought less and less. Everyone was handsome and talented, but I unceremoniously pushed his face in the pillow and thought, 'Bite that and shut up.' I listened intently for any sighs from behind me, deep breathing or pounding. But Omar never made a noise, and I had no idea what he was doing or thinking. It didn't matter in a way. The important thing was that he was there. After a time I found I couldn't make headway unless he was. Anyone I met by myself and brought back proved an abysmal humiliation, as if Omar had jinxed my own efforts, and made me dependent on his.

Was he trying to win me over from the man he had picked up for me? Touting and being rewarded in terms other than monetary? What a refreshing change! Hitherto it had always been the age-old principle – No dosh, no dick: no cash, no cunt. Was I at last entering a higher plain?

I knew sooner or later I'd commit the forbidden, and spy on Omar as he stood behind me. If I'd turned round, if our eyes had met, everything would have been over. No use placing a mirror on the pillow. From certain angles glasses could act as mirrors, in particular cheap sunglasses with protective spray on only one side of the lenses. I went through scenarios, laughed at the thought of glasses steaming up. Eventually I found some surgical goggles that protected the eye from dust and infection after an operation. They were odd-looking things but could without suspicion be adapted to reflect. I told Omar I had to wear them at all times because of an eye infection. A condom for the eyes, I joked.

I was now about to see what had made me slip anchor and skip work, and exhaust myself and think only of the knock on the door. I was to see a hitherto unseen presence. It was a transgression point, of course, and invited punishment, like Actaeon seeing Diana, or Lohengrin being asked his name. Something in me said, Leave things, leave Omar, alone. Let him keep his agenda private. If he goes off to do his own thing, with us on his mind, so what?

Vanity, or the opposite, drove me on. What could he see in me? What did I prompt him to do? I could feel his presence wishing me, well-wishing me on. I never sensed his eyes drilling the back of my head, but I sometimes thought he cupped his palms over my compressed and pounding butt cheeks and pushed me forward and in ever harder and deeper.

The surgical glasses did not give a particularly clear view of him. It resembled the fleeting vision of a man seen through the fog, or the steam of the shower room, glimpsed momentarily in the dark, a suggestion from behind, not full frontal. He stood by a gap in the curtains, in the flickering light. He didn't move or touch himself, and there was no evidence of a bulge. He remained poised and enrapt, the thought of what was going on more stimulating than ever taking part, pent to the point of self-combustion. He could only see the rear, but perhaps imagined what was happening in front.

Which, of course, recalled what that stupid Leroy often said. He claimed he could mentally undress a man, size him up, tell at a glance if he were circumcised, even when he'd last had sex. What an idiot that man was! He got all his kicks from what he called a brain orgasm, a mind-fuck to you and me.

On his reckoning my first sight of Omar standing behind me should have been sufficient. But I felt my usual certainties giving way and needing continual confirmation. For over a week I wore the surgical goggles. My vision of him grew clearer. Had Omar known I'd seen him he would undoubtedly have left for good. As it was, he acted as if he could be seen, and played to the audience. He always arrived in everyday clothes, carrying a suitcase. By the time he stood behind me he had changed into the height of fashion, or as if he was modelling sports gear – which face-to-face and in the cold light of day, I would've doubted he could carry off. But there he was, looking the part, outrivalling and giving flesh to men I had so drooled over in photos. He had dressed up, unseen by any-one, but almost claiming 'I could do, but I don't choose to.'

My excuse of a bad eye could not be sustained for more than a week or so. What I had seen, albeit imperfectly, was implanted in my mind, but could only be conjured up in Omar's unseen presence. And then it took wing. I would undress him, dress him up, put him through every bizarre and imaginable hoop.

I'd never been given to such imaginings before, to the sensuous, the erotic, let alone the sensitive. I had thought them mere delaying tactics, such as courting and foreplay. Deadening influences, necrotic. Now, it was as if something had been peeled off, and my old raw appetites held in check.

I paused between one precipitate action and the next. I was more detached and reflective. I ceased pouring over porn, and spent much time in art galleries. I walked straight past the Caravaggio, and spent hours contemplating Correggio. Both Hadley and Leroy thought I was having some meaningful and mysterious affair that had softened me. It was not like that at all. It was more layered. I let them go on thinking what they liked.

Both Omar and I had changed. Omar, the guardian angel who thought it took three to make a marriage was no longer that third party. The link was between him and me.

As to the endless pick-ups he brought round, nothing changed there. They existed for one purpose only. I never spoke to them. I pushed them face downward into the pillow, parted their cheeks and spat. And it was a matter of indifference to me if their death-honk was on feathers or kapok.

I never asked them to stay or come back. But the minute they had gone another layer of erotic fantasy began. I rose to the poetic precept – poetry, I ask you! – of 'drama recalled in tranquillity.' I went to a quiet dark corner, and succumbed to an irresistible vision. A wank after the event, I think it's called.

Actaeon

I COULD NEVER WORK OUT WHY the Ancient Romans made Diana both the goddess of hunting and an emblem of chastity. Surely the two are mutually exclusive. Now, if the Christians had done this I could have seen, if not understood, how it might slot into their dualistic outlook. Not a profound thought, perhaps. The sort that often came to me at the end of a long day, and which I took for significant, but was later to rethink.

It was a full moon. I sat on a bench in the park, reflecting on the days' events, collecting my thoughts and putting them in some sort of order, a necessary reaction to the strains of life at the Ministry. Several of my colleagues held the world at bay by scribbling in a diary, last thing at night. A senior colleague claimed it was therapeutic and levelled out the peaks and troughs of existence – or as he said, or rather sang 'Every valley shall be exalted, and the high places made low'. Another was convinced that in years to come a diary might provide an insight into current political events. He was unnaturally secretive about the diary's contents, claiming they'd never be published till after his death. I started to keep one, but quickly gave up. I couldn't see the point. I was happy just to sit on the side-lines observing, a little niche on the periphery.

I often came here, to the edge of the trolling area. I noted the arrivals, the erstwhile dog walkers, the pretend joggers. We all knew what brought us here. In those days it was one of the few places my sort could go. I was on nodding acquaintance with many of the regulars. I watched them dive into the wood, and later emerge accompanied – or more often alone, some striding ten foot tall, the majority morose with hang-dog expressions. A few never surfaced, as if engulfed in a whirlpool. For me, it was vicarious pleasure. I rarely ventured under the trees myself. I stood vigil, like the hand-maiden Brangaene, and listened to the distant sounds of cars, like off-stage hunting horns.

Naturally, I never let on at the Ministry. I couldn't afford to, not even if I'd been older, higher up and established. I was Chief Adviser to the Junior Minister at the Home Office, Sir Godfrey Chesham. He'd inherited the title, not earned it. But as he always quipped to new staff 'It's better you call me 'Sir Godfrey' rather than 'Mr Chesham, sir.' More familiar. Even though I've never met you before you can call me by my Christian name from the start.'

He was, of course, a Christian. He thought himself a manly pillar, upright and proper, who'd always give weight to the right side, and respond to the call. Yet he had a worldly streak and often said 'Oh the poor! They'll always be with us. If they weren't there could be no Charity.' Accordingly, he imbibed freely, gorged himself, and rode to hounds.

I was careful not to get on the wrong side of him. He

expected a lot from his junior colleagues, and when faced with objections would shout 'Brazen it out – like a man.' I couldn't complain. From the start he'd taken me under his wing, possibly because I did most of his work, which he was all too happy to offload. I dealt with day-to-day routines and trained new staff, but my main rôle was what would later be called a trouble-shooter. I kept his appointment book – and made excuses when he didn't turn up to an important function. I drew up feasibility reports, always mindful to emphasise the not inconsiderable snags involved in even the most minor changes. Above all, I drafted replies to parliamentary questions. A well-researched answer can scotch a spiky question. A wise precaution, as the current Opposition Spokesman was sharper than most, and definitely out for blood.

Sir Godfrey was grateful for my efforts. He kept asking me to come down to his country house and go hunting with him, which I wasn't very keen to do. He suggested I go down to his constituency to help with some local difficulties. I pointed out that as a Civil Servant I couldn't get involved in party political matters. 'Nonsense,' he'd exclaim, adding that he might be able to get me a safe seat at the next election. 'You'd have to get yourself a wife though.'

I liked the idea of becoming an MP. It wasn't a career to be sneezed at. I'd learnt a lot about procedures. The idea of Service appealed to me. Something Roman. Pro bono publico. I don't think my concept of being an MP would've been the same as Sir Godfrey's. Anyhow, it was unlikely to happen. The Government wasn't popular, and few constituencies could be called safe.

Though, of course, Sir Godfrey's was. 'You must come down. Only an hour out of London. Could be another world. Got a sense of history – and liberty.' And he'd tell me a great length of the Battle of Lewes and how Simon de Montfort had won our liberties on that critical day in 1264, the 700th Anniversary of which was due in less than ten years time. 'God willing, I'll still be around to celebrate it.'

I smiled, and assured him he would be. Frankly I was dubious about De Montfort's supposed aim of establishing parliamentary freedom. Baronial privileges, more like. However, I didn't press the point.

I bore Sir Godfrey's suggestion in mind. It was tempting and often resurfaced unbidden after a hard day carrying out his work. If I had a constituency of my own I'd have the excuse to leave London each weekend, enjoy fresh air and country life. That would be better than coming here – which is not something I could ever risk if I were an MP. But until that happens I must snatch what free time I can. I need my stolen hour, to unwind at the end of the day, in the open.

When the moon comes out from the clouds it unveils a magic glade. The pools of silver light contrast with the dark clumps of bushes. The paths are so well-trodden that the roots of the overhanging trees are exposed.

Should I do a circuit or two, just to see what was going on? To see, that is, in the sense of the lie of the land. Not as a looker or voyeur. Of course, you get them here. They annoy me intensely. Why don't they leave people alone? It's the last thing I ever want to be accused of. If inadvertently I ever disturb a couple at play I always apologise and move off quickly. I've never gained satisfaction from muscling in and taking over.

I snaked my way under the trees, avoiding the main path and walking on the tufts of grass to prevent treading on dry twigs. I felt elevated, enervated, invisible, grateful that such a place existed. I went into a reverie and lost all sense of direction. I turned round and round to re-orientate. I could see the main path clearly through the trees. No panic. I just needed to push by a large clump of bushes, then cut across the grass.

I noticed a couple against a tree-trunk on the left. I didn't want to turn back and go the long route to avoid them. There was surely enough space to slip by. I tip-toed as if tracking an animal. I hadn't reckoned on the exposed roots. I tripped. I must have muttered something as I righted myself. The man on his knees got up and turned towards me. I froze. The moon came out from behind the clouds – and confirmed – it was Sir Godfrey. For a moment I wanted to laugh in surprise and say 'Fancy seeing you here!' But no. The look on his face was like thunder. A portcullis came down. My voice went. I couldn't even mutter an apology. I moved back into the trees and away from the path. I walked straight home, fighting off the possibility I'd seen him. How could it be him? Surely not. Similarities perhaps. No, not even that. I'd never seen him give a look quite like that.

The next morning I got to the Office early, determined to behave as if nothing had happened. Sir Godfrey was there already, which was quite unheard of. He greeted me ebulliently.

'Surprised to see me, eh?' He paused as if waiting for an answer. 'Won't happen again.' He smiled and slapped me on the shoulder. 'Lucky to see me at all – today.'

He then told me at great length how he'd spent all the previous evening with his wife at the ballet.

'Bloody long it was. God, did it go on!'

'Oh, yes,' I said, trying to fit in with his tone. 'What was it you saw?'

'Don't even ask. They're all the same. Load of pansies prancing round with padded balls. Not my cup of tea at all. I only go for the wife. If I can skip an act and stay in the Crush Bar I will. If not, well, I've always got a bottle in the box. Couldn't wait for the meal afterwards. Went to Simpson's. The Carvery. Can't beat a good roast. Bit late for a meal, though. Ate too much. Kept me awake most of the night. Thought I might as well come in early as not. Won't happen often.'

He paused and looked at the pile of work on my desk. 'Don't feel like doing much today,' he said and disappeared.

I rejoiced the encounter was over so soon. There were possible hidden meanings to his words, but nothing to cause offence. He hadn't asked me what I'd been doing. I put the suspicion from my mind and set to work.

By evening I was exhausted. A meal out seemed appropriate. I phoned to book a table at a favourite haunt and slowly made my way there. I could have done with time to myself, but I was spotted. Of all people by an old flame, Bertrand. I always try to avoid him now. He buttonholeth, and doth give the Ear-ache. Today for some reason I felt drawn to him.

'Can't stop long,' he said.

His second home is the Opera House. He never says Covent Garden.

'I'm off the Garden.'

He never says Don Giovanni.

'I'm off to the Don '

He never says the Magic Flute.

'Have you seen the new Flute? Queen of the Night's a gem. Spot on with those high Fs. You must go. Don't suppose you'll get tickets, though.'

I mentioned I'd been very busy lately, but added that my boss had gone to the Ballet yesterday.

'Can't have, darling. This season they're not doing Mondays. Sounds like a tart, doesn't it? "Don't do mornings, luv." It gives them longer to set up the scenery. They're doing far more productions this season. Have you booked for Die Frau …? Hasn't been done for twenty years. Last saw it at the Vienna Opera. Had to stand right at the back of the gods. You know how high up that is. And me with my vertigo! It was a dream cast. Then one of the principals dropped out. Luckily the replacement was even better. And …'

I'd ceased listening. So Sir Godfrey couldn't have been at the ballet yesterday. He had lied. Nothing unusual in politics. But why? If he wasn't at the ballet where was he? So, it could've been him in the park. Not necessarily though. But if so … So what? I left it at that.

Sir Godfrey was in early the following morning.

'Things can't go like this,' he chortled. 'Look. I've been

thinking. I've probably been overworking you. Don't want you to crack up or anything. Start getting delusions or – seeing things. How'd it be if I got that new bloke to help you out? Seems pleasant enough, doesn't he?'

'Depends what it is,' I replied dubiously. 'There's some quite routine stuff I could hand over.'

'I was thinking perhaps he could take over drafting the answers to the parliamentary questions.'

I didn't like that idea at all. Researching the answers gave a real insight into ministerial responsibilities, and was valuable experience should I ever become an MP.

'I'd rather not, Sir Godfrey. As you know … the Government's going through a rough patch. And …'

'And?'

I looked straight into his eyes and said, 'Someone might ask you a tricky question.'

A slight cloud passed over his face. 'Wouldn't want that, would we?' he said quickly. 'Think that makes my point for me, though. You need an extra pair of hands. I'll ask that new chap. Test his mettle. You be his adviser till he gets in his stride. In the meantime you might like to take over some of his work. Choose the easy stuff. Don't overdo it.'

I did as requested. Little else I could do. He never repeated his invitation to visit his constituency, and never mentioned the safe seat. I couldn't worry. There'd been a change of cast at the Ministry. There'd probably be a change of Government at the election. I rather hoped so. I might end up working for the shadow Home Office Minister – who was decidedly more on the ball than Sir

Godfrey.

The work load proved just as great, but far less demanding, and no longer absorbed my attention. I felt freer, slightly cussed, and more inclined to round off the day sitting in the park.

It was a full moon, and must have been exactly a month since my abortive sighting of Sir Godfrey. Totally cloudless it was, a beautiful evening, just what I needed. I sat on my usual seat and nodded to the regulars. There weren't so many about, which was surprising for a moonlit night.

Then out of nowhere two men appeared and stood in front of me. One put his hand in his pocket. I thought he was going to pull out a weapon. He showed me a card.

'Police. We're arresting you for indecency.'

'But …'

'No buts, sir. Just come along quietly. We're merely enforcing the law.'

'Yes,' the second man added, 'and you know what the law is, don't you, sir? You work in the Home Office and make them.'

'How can you know …?'

'Please don't resist,' the first man interrupted. 'That'll only make it worse.'

'But I wasn't doing any…'

Of course, that's not what they asserted next morning in court. I've never seen such a packed court. I couldn't believe the public gallery normally got that full. Both officers swore on the Bible that they'd caught me in a public place, under the trees, with another man, committing an act of gross indecency. The other man was too quick for them but, because I had my trousers round my ankles, I was unable to make such a speedy getaway. The public gallery, which hitherto had been tut-tutting in disapproval, now burst into hoots of laughter – and the judge saw fit to adjourn the case till the following week.

That weekend the Home Secretary himself intervened in a long and well-publicised speech.

'This is not a laughing matter. This is serious, as few things are. This strikes at the very heart of all the values we cherish in our society. We are not going to let this pass with a grin or a shrug. This evil has wormed its way into the highest echelons. Thankfully through the vigilance of my staff we have been able to identify and root out this pestilence.

'And just as we have routed it from our place of work I ask you all as decent, law-abiding citizens to do the same at your place of work, in the street you live in, at – God forbid – the school you send your innocent children to. If need be in your own family.'

The dogs were unleashed. The hunt was on. Sir Godfrey was put in charge.

I received a prison sentence commensurate with grievous bodily harm. I had the right of appeal, but with little prospect of success. I could've said I'd seen Sir Godfrey in the park. To what avail? It was a month ago. I had no proof. No-one would've believed me.

By chance I did I end up making a visit to his constituency. I was taken to Lewes prison, one of the worst run in the country, a grim eyesore on the edge of that pleasant town. His local jail. Almost as if I was his personal prisoner. Detained there at his pleasure.

Naturally, I was separated from the other prisoners. They made clear they didn't go in for what I was accused of. I didn't miss out by being isolated. I was given access to all the newspapers. They had a field day. Out to get anyone like me and my followers. I never realised before that I had followers. Now I acquired – my ilk, my sort, my persuasion, my like, my type. The attacks weren't just in newsprint. There were daily reports of inflammatory speeches in parliament and pulpits, police surveillance, provocation and arrests. It was vicious. Gloves off. Many people were clobbered. Locked up. Sent into hiding. No knowing how many.

The campaign made the Government far more popular. They won a couple of by-elections and decided to hold an early general election, which they won. Sir Godfrey increased his majority in Lewes – I was not entitled to vote – and he was promoted to Chief Secretary to the Treasury.

A few months later I was quietly let out. Even with remission for good conduct it was premature. There were no reporters at the gate. No transport. And, of course, no prospects. A prison sentence meant I was automatically disqualified from a post in public service. A conviction for my particular 'crime' barred the doors to most other jobs. Once the cover was blown we had no more chance than spies or grouse. I sold up, salvaged what I could, and went on my travels. Little else I could do.

I met several other exiles, including Bertrand. He only got as far as the French coast, from which he stared back morosely. I kept going South, for a time toying with a change of name, getting married, scribbling it out my system, despising myself for not staying to fight the good fight. I'd lost all belief that a life in public service could change the world. I barely followed the newspaper headlines. Of course, I was delighted when I heard that Sir Godfrey had proved a disaster at the Treasury, and had been kicked upstairs to the Lords. But that didn't alter much.

In time, in the warm South, I found a foothold, settled in with local customs. Years passed and I heard that things had changed for the better, as if a dictator had been overthrown. People were asking about me. I would be welcomed back as some sort of suffering celebrity.

I wasn't keen. One bitten, twice shy. I knew, as an insider, that the backwoods could always regroup. It's no great mental leap for them to reconcile the goddess of hunting and the goddess of chastity; the Chaste Diana being but a precursor to the Virgin Mary.

I've grown used to the antic magic of archaeological sites by moonlight. Gardens recreated in the ancient style. Statues in arbours. Herms in grottoes. Supplicants embracing the knees of victors.

Dryads live in this pagan grove, scantily clothed in olive green, with a glint of gold and mottled as a faun.

Tell me. Is he statue? Or is he real? Bronzed as terracotta certainly.

Foot Script

MY ILLNESSES HAVE RARELY BEEN of a physical nature. Nothing of the romantic leg or arm breaks incurred in sport or even accident. I almost wish I'd been on the receiving end. It certainly creates attention and admiration. I'd often played – is that the right word? – along with this, signing my name on the plaster cast on the leg of a schoolboy athlete I fancied. On the other hand, nowadays, when out for a walk in the park I might look on eagerly at the footballers, but I always develop a sudden limp if the ball comes my way. My whole make-up has always been geared for some indefinable, slow-developing, implacably-advancing malaise that has nothing to do with the desire to compete with or outdo other people.

My outlook changed when something physical did happen to me. One day whilst on my pedestrian rounds I felt a sudden click in my ankle. Had I broken it, twisted it, ricked it, dislocated it? It could have been any of these. It also turned out to be a Eureka click, a positive snap of the fingers and thumbs.

The pain, however, was genuine and it showed on my face and in my movements. I received many offers of help. I was proffered a supporting arm and hopped towards a recently-vacated seat. I was helped upstairs, across the road, on and off buses.

'Poor you. How did you do that?'

I know full well I wouldn't have been offered help – let alone sympathy – if I'd been out jay-walking, or talking to myself, or lying in the gutter playing the zither on the drain. Or even barking at a dog.

'I had something similar myself,' my comforters said. 'You should see a doctor.'

Should I? I tried the internet first, which gave advice and a list of exercises, all of which I carried out conscientiously enough, but to little avail. The time did indeed come to see a doctor. He gave much the same advice; rest, anti-inflammatories, surgical stockings, gentle exercise, and he added, cheerily, 'a bag of frozen peas. You can still eat them later. And they don't have to be minted. See you next month.'

I did all he suggested in good faith – incidentally I bought a bag of petit pois – and walked round the block, up and down stairs, etc., again to little avail. On my return visit the doctor shrugged and said 'I can refer you to a physio. Very good on sport injuries.'

The Physio was young, fit and smelt of shower gel. I'd have happily signed my name on a plaster cast on any part of his body he might choose to break or strain, sealed it with a kiss even. He confirmed the doctor's advice. 'No X-ray yet. More Exercise.' He didn't rule out a future appointment might be necessary. He sent the appropriate exercises by email. Pages of them, with day-by-day tables to fill in. The exercises themselves were much the same as before, except for one which claimed that the single best exercise for moving the ankle in all directions was to pretend to write each letter of the alphabet. A true revelation! I never supposed physiotherapists could be so literary!

My handwriting had deteriorated from excess dependence on the computer keyboard and I soon saw the efficacy of forming the letters with my foot. The whole alphabet, beginning to end. I started with capitals because they were straight lines. It was like going back to infant school. A BA CA DER EFF FER. I soon progressed to lower case, initially without crossing the t's and dotting the i's. Eventually I graduated to join-ups. It revived my literary ambitions. Incidentally it was my right ankle I was exercising, but I was actually left-handed. My whole bodily co-ordination had improved. I had become silently ambidextrous.

Of course, I attempted only short words to start with. I would sit downstairs on a bus and endure someone shouting into a hands-free mobile phone and, without my face registering or my hands moving, I could discreetly give rein to my thoughts with my right foot. 'Shush.' In shops I would smile a thanks, stand on my left leg while the right ankle tattooed 'Short weight-givers.'

Longer words followed, as when I had to avoid someone jaywalking the pavement, absorbed in his mobile phone, both thumbs on the keypad. I'd always thought that having a separate thumb had hastened

Evolution in favour of Humans. I now rather doubted it. I drummed out 'You Colossal Thicko.'

You – in a derogatory and accusatory sense – was to became a prominent word. If a jogger came up from behind, huffing and puffing germs all over me, I'd head for the nearest park bench and morse code the words 'Drop dead.' In time this was to develop into 'Why don't you bloody well fuck off and die.'

Sometimes I'd be sitting on a park bench and a dog would bounce up and sniff round. I'd say to the owner 'Lovely dog you've got there.' And my ankle would write 'Piss up someone else's leg.' And interestingly the dog instinctively understood in a way it's dozy owner never could have done. It skipped off merrily and found a car-wheel.

How nice it was to maintain the social graces outwardly, but express real thoughts, both inwardly – and physically. Nice, also, to have both a physical illness and a new form of expression that fitted in with my natural inventiveness. I had much to thank the Physio for. I was not just a static recipient of his ministrations, but had been given a gift to develop. I looked forward to seeing him again.

I continued to extend my vocabulary, developing a wide range of unusual responses. I even made words up. I was intent on upgrading the lesser-used consonants and limiting the use of vowels, save, as in the case of i and u and the semi-vowel y, when they could be doubled. These made-up words didn't need to be pronounced; they could be alternatively spelt and they didn't necessarily have to mean anything. Well, so what? Frankly over the years I'd been called a variety of derogatory words – wally, nerd, berk, pillock, prat – and I'd never been sure what any of them actually meant. There was no reason why I shouldn't be proud of my own inventions.

Of course, to do justice to my new lexicon and to practise the articulation of my foot I needed time each day for quiet reflection. I found a secluded park bench, discreetly away from the circuit of most joggers. It had been a long journey, a positive learning curve, a physically exhausting exercise routine. And the month was not even up before I had the option of seeing the Physio again. I had achieved much. A new confidence – that I wasn't letting any imagined slight pass without comment, and also that there would be no adverse comeback from that comment. I had found my voice. I almost began to mellow, even to wonder if I hadn't over-reacted in the past, lacked understanding, mistaken motives, got the wrong end of the stick. I began to feel substantial, appreciate my own weight, my avoir-du-pois and gravitas. Perhaps it was true what pundits had said, that sport releases tensions and even helps contain hostility and prevents it escalating.

I looked up from my deliberations and saw a jogger running in my direction. Time was when I'd have cursed him for spoiling my reverie. But what was there to find objectionable in this simple uncomplicated exercise? In skimpy shorts and T-shirt, he was. Oh. And strangely familiar. Not to be avoided or mistaken. No! It can't be. It was. And coming straight towards the bench I was sitting on. My gorgeous Physio. My Saviour. He, who had put me on the right road. I sat to attention and frantically began to signal with my right ankle.

Remember me? I am your best student. Your personal best. Thanks to you – and you alone – my ankle is cured – more than cured. Not grown wings yet but …

He accelerated. And ran straight past, without acknowledging me, or looking my way, just lobbing something into the waste-bin alongside the bench.

I hope he felt the full force of the tsunami of expletives my foot machine-gunned in his direction. Bastard was the mildest.

Nil-Nihil

I CAN THINK OF NOTHING ELSE. I am so looking forward to meeting him again. And for the last time. And in such circumstances! We will shake hands formally at the beginning of The Game – and then at the end, I, as captain of the winning side, will, as part of the victory celebrations, ceremonially hang him from the goal post.

I know I should not be writing this or showing any special feelings, but it does not imply I am unaware of the Rules or doubt their validity. They are quite clear and state – the winning team has the right to hang the losing team. It is a good rule; and since it has been instituted has proved beneficial for The Game and has improved personal performances. The enhanced results look most impressive in the Achievement Record Books.

WIN or DIE is the motto of the Game. The winners bask in the praise of the crowd, humbly accept the prizes presented by the Reigning Powers and carry out all stages of the Celebrations, of which the climax is The Hanging.

Everyone accepts the Rules, including the losing side. It is dishonourable to try and escape the inevitable, to cheat by killing yourself or inducing a fatal heart attack. Any call for mercy by the losing players and the crowd will chant 'You pussies' – and demand the winning team mutilate them alive. We would normally only mutilate

after The Hanging as symbolic acts in token of and
respect for The Game itself. Legs are broken and feet
severed; the goalkeeper's hands are chopped off. The
genitals are cut off and forced down the throat as revenge
for any verbal abuse and disrespect shown to the winning
side. If a captain of a losing team were to show cowardice,
or beg for mercy for himself or for his team, he would be
dealt with even more severely, and decapitated and his
head kicked across the playing field and into the goal he
had failed to defend.

Sometimes cowardice occurs within the winning team.
I once had to intervene and use my rights as Captain
when a player from our side, fearing we would lose,
deliberately fouled an opponent. I had no alternative but
to push the player through the boundary phalanx of lines-
men into the Area of Limbo where he was immediately
beheaded and 'piked' for all to see. We won that game.
There were ten victors to hang eleven losers. I had the
honour of hanging, or as it is known, necking, two
opponents.

The Rules can be modified in certain circumstances,
for example regarding the quality of play. If the game has
been particularly exciting then only the losing captain is
necked, the decision is the spectators. The rest of the
losing team have their hamstrings cut or their feet drilled.
They become Muckers, clearing away bodies and sluicing
down the stadium. The mark of failure is on them for as
long as they are allowed to live.

If the match ends in a draw then the two sides fight to
the death and to the last man. We take on the rival
position, captain to captain, striker to striker. We have no

weapons and most often dispatch our opponent with a rabbit punch, or by throttling with bent arms. Kicking is another approved method. We must never intervene in any ongoing combat. That is the affair of each particular position. However, if the victor in the adjacent position is from the opposing team then we are expected to take him on. It is important to think of the pitch squared out in this way.

My former best friend – no, I must not talk in terms of friends, they are not permissible in The Game – taught me a lot when we played on the same side. He encouraged me before my first necking. I was squeamish. 'Go down that road,' he said, 'and you'll become a Pacifist, and we know what happens to them.' He demonstrated the best technique of dispatch. 'Embrace the legs, like so, lift up the body as high as you can, then drop it. Listen for the rewarding click. Sounds like a kiss.' He was right and I thank him for it. He is now captain of the rival team we play this weekend. I will have to hang him. 'Look at his face as you lift him,' he used to say, 'and think you'd do the same for me if I lost.' True. And I will. Without compunction. It will sound like the kiss I could never give him. The thought excites me even now.

The winning captain can claim the wife and goods of the defeated captain. Also, the dead captain's male children can be put to death as potential future rivals. With my friend I'll not dishonour his wife. I have no wish to make contact with her. I will kill her along with his all children.

I should have mentioned the fact that before The Hanging – I am in a bit of a quandary about this as there

may be a change in the order of service – comes The
Fucking. Each team has eleven cheerleaders. They are
trained in Special Schools to show no interest in anything
but The Game, and no loyalty other than their own team.
They are kept as virgins and cheer on their teams during
the course of the match. The winning team publicly fucks
the cheerleaders of the losing team. The cheerleaders
know their fate – the risks and rewards – and still come
forward. The supply is endless.

The procedure for The Fucking is as follows. At the
end of the game the winning players are given a glucose
drink and fitted with a condom. The cheerleaders of the
losing team are led on to the squared-out pitch, each
square now double in size as we have claimed the territory
of the losing side. The hands of the cheerleaders are tied
together, but not their legs.

Then the Rhythm begins. This is a rudimentary form
of music pumped out full blast. It is not played with instruments, but is synthesised percussive sound, inter-
spersed with barnyard noises. All the supporters, even
those of the defeated team, chant obscenities.

The Fucking never lasts more than ten minutes. I
never like to be the first or last to finish. About the third
or fourth I think is the best timing. Our own cheerleaders
ceremonially remove the condoms and hold them up to
show the crowd that we have cum. If a Player claims to
have cum, and has, in fact, not done so, he will be ridiculed to the point of suicide. This rarely happens, but is
always a fear. Our cheerleaders then ensure the condom
is sealed, labelled and sent to a secret location, not even
marked on military maps. Anyone approaching within ten

kilometres of the secret compound – even by accident – will be shot. The sperm is frozen and sold to the highest global bidder.

We are then washed down by our own cheerleaders, who take the opportunity to spit and kick at the recently-fucked cheerleaders of the losing side and call them all manner of slags and sluts. Sometimes if the fucked women are fainting from exhaustion our cheerleaders will throw the filthy soapy water in their faces. Their legs are now tied together, and, according to the whim of the spectators, these defiled cheerleaders are either killed out-right – which is the preferred choice of the majority of cheerleaders themselves – or, still living, taken as play-things to twilight homes for elderly supporters of the winning team.

When we players have been fully cleaned and per-fumed we are dressed in robes and escorted to the podium and listen to the speeches from the Powers. We are then presented with our prizes, before returning to the pitch for the ceremonial Hangings, as previously described.

As I say the order of service may change. Personally, I am happy that the Prize-Giving precedes The Hanging. I think it is much easier to hang my opponent when I have received a medal giving me identity and entitlement. However, I am not so sure that The Hanging should precede The Fucking. Procedural changes are always the most unsettling.

Incidentally, there is also a proposal to introduce a central scaffold, quickly erected at the end of the game, to use for both the Prize-Giving and the Hangings. At present The Hanging takes place on the cross bar of the goal. The goalposts have to be extended and reinforced to take the weight of the eleven men. First, the net is unhitched and laid flat, so as not to obscure the view. It is also used to pile the bodies on and drag them off when they are cut down. The side posts are raised hydraulically and hooks are clipped to the crossbar. Each hook can twist through 360 degrees so the body can be spun round for all to see. Personally, I can see nothing wrong with the present arrangement. I like the sense of intruding into the territory of the opponent.

The reasoning behind the proposed central scaffold is to give better sightlines, in particular for the supporters of the losing team. They will see more clearly and should be chastened by the hanging of their team, and thus learn the hard way – that losing does not pay. This is good in theory. In point of fact, I have noticed that many of the supporters of the defeated team lose all sense of loyalty and cheer along with the winning supporters as each player is dispatched.

When the ceremonies are over the spectators leave the stadium and return to the streets. They divide into rival gangs and begin killing each other. Mistakes are made and they kill many of their own side. The killing frenzy often reaches genocidal proportions. This is known as the Self-Cull and is a good method of reducing the population. When the Security Forces feel the Self-Cull has achieved its aim and does not endanger the Work Quota (some-times called the Minimum Necessary Labour Force), the survivors are made to clear up and dispose of the bodies. Fork-lift trucks, digging machines and snow ploughs are used. Many bodies are crushed flat under the large wheels or caterpillar tracks. Relatives cannot claim the bodies of anyone killed in street riots. There are no enquiries or appeals.

Yet despite the rivalry between teams, supporters are united in one thing – the importance of The Game itself. They express this most strongly in their hatred of non-participants, people who do not support any team, non-combatants. They are called Pacifists. They come forward in columns, unarmed save for protest banners. No-one knows where they come from or what their real motivation is, but the supply is limitless. They are rounded up each week and taken to the stadium for public execution. Supporters of The Game can pay to kill a batch of five. The queues for this are often longer than for tickets for a match. There can be few loyal supporters who have not at one time or another put paid to the subversive non-combat of a Pacifist. At Training School we were regularly given a quota to dispatch by different methods. We were never allowed to use our guns, and I understand that guns are not allowed in the stadium culls in case they are used against the Security Forces. Supporters have to devise other ways of killing their quota. They bring in knives, pieces of wood, lengths of rope and wire. The favourite chant – presumably on the basis that anyone who is not prepared to kill is incapable of doing much else – is 'Pacifists can't fuck.' After the killing the supporters go off to a prostitute. A supporter once confided to me 'After a morning of killing I was so excited and pent up that I came the moment I penetrated her.'

I have never attended one of these events myself but, as a Team Captain, I am entitled to act as an independent observer to ensure that all the proceedings are carried out thoroughly and without any show of mercy, and also that the Stadium is sluiced down by the Muckers in readiness for the match.

It has taken me a long time to get to the position of Captain. Once or twice I have played in the losing team, fortunately when the crowd did not thumbs-down the whole team but only the captain. I have matured as The Game itself has grown in importance. The Powers approve of it as a form of social control. It is a compulsory subject at school and is quickly replacing all other subjects. Officials scout the back streets on the look-out for talented players, who are taken to Special Schools, run by each team. Once registered in the Special School you have no further contact with your relatives, and are allowed no visits and no communication with the outside world. The discipline is stricter than in a top-security prison. We are discouraged from holding or expressing an opinion other than the official one. We are not taught to write except our name. This is for contracts and autographs. We receive no other formal education. Some of us may have had prior learning. We are discouraged from further learning on our own. My own ability to write would – if known – certainly count against me. There must be others who can write. My friend was not among them. His only interest was in The Game. He never responded when I told him I could write – and I often did so.

On being registered in the School we are organized

into groups and compete among ourselves. Only later do we have matches with Schools run by other teams. Our only outing, not directly concerned with The Game, is the Initiation Fuck, arranged for us on our twelfth birthday. We are left in a lighted room with a blinded concubine. Her blindness is a liberation, and allows us to explore and experiment without inhibition. Then we graduate to sex in darkened rooms with sighted prostitutes, and then – once we are playing rival teams in the Main Stadium – to the public Fucking of the cheerleaders of the defeated team.

As Players we are obliged to marry. But this is only nominal. Should we wish to visit a prostitute we have Diplomatic Immunity and are expected to kill her immediately afterwards. We used to blind them and cut out their tongues, but this merely created a vagrancy problem so the rule was changed – and, in this case, as in so many others, I agree with the Powers. I have found a way of using these rules for my own benefit. The only time I can be totally alone with my own thoughts is with a prostitute. It is the only time I can write. I always kill the prostitute first and spend the allotted time writing. In case the body is checked I masturbate into a condom and push it up her.

I write to take stock. I know the match this weekend will be the climax of my career. After I have won against my friend's team, after I have necked him, with no show of regret whatever, whatever my inner feelings may be, I will retire as a Player and go on to the next stage. There are several possible avenues. We can be selected as a Personal Trainer to the wives of one of the Powers. Such an invitation – and its inevitable call to the bedroom – cannot be refused. We may also be expected to get rid of the husband. This can be tricky as an embryonic system of laws operates among the Powers. Public killing and fucking are unheard of among them. Everything is done in private.

Some Players go on to be Referees, but the majority become Trainers in the Special Schools. Grooms we call them. That is not my personal preference, though, of course, the decision does not rest with me. Several former Players end up as Commentators. Glossatores is the word. It is an honourable profession – they are taught the basic elements of the language and the vocabulary necessary for The Game – and become wise and venerable men acting either as psychologists, who assess the players; as prophets, who foretell the results of a game; as educators, or as Keepers of the Scripts, who compile the Achievement Record Book, which is learned by heart in all Special Schools. I am not myself very interested in these particular areas. However, there is one function of the Glossatores that would interest me. They can also act as Legal Advisors who revise the Rules of The Game. Here I have definite opinions. There are many current practices and proposed changes I would, if asked, strongly question.

For instance, selected players of top quality but from different teams often merge and take on teams from other countries. Some of these countries have different rules. They do not let us hang all the defeated team, or sometimes only just the captain. Or they use another method of execution. In one country no killing is permitted at all! Again, I think the rules should be standardised and our particular practices universally adopted.

Similarly, there are some countries which do not even play The Game. Naturally, we intervene. If there is the slightest protest or opposition we take over the whole country, and The Game is made compulsory. The child population of that country is given just as much food or medicine as is required to play The Game. Promising players are brought back to our Special Schools. Again, I think that our practices – and not the laxer ones of other countries – should be globally enforced.

However, there is one proposal by the Powers – being kicked around from committee to committee and verbally commented on by some Glossatores – which worries me greatly. This is to change the order of the Winning Ceremony. Is it better to have the Hanging before or after the Fucking? I know I keep coming back to this, but it concerns us Players more than is perhaps realised. On one level it is a simple question – do we need light relief before the Hanging? Or would the supporters of the vanquished team be still more chastened after the Hanging to see its cheerleaders publicly degraded? Everything is effect – and result. The Powers only seem concerned with the reaction of the crowd. I can understand this to an extent, but they have been wrongly advised; crucial facts are not being taken into consideration. For example, if the Hanging comes last then violence will be on the minds of the spectators and they will leave the stadium and the Population Cull will happen as normal. However, if the Fucking comes last then the crowd may go out and the result could be, not a reduction in population, but an increase! It is a finely balanced decision and could have implications on the numbers filling the stadium, even on the numbers of players, cheerleaders and pacifists. All these groups are perfectly reconciled to their fate and permanently insurging; any significant increase in supply could spell disaster.

The proposed change is anyway based on a false premise. Having the Fucking first does not imply precedence over the Hanging. Having the Hanging last does not imply it is the climax of the proceedings. The two are equal. We have always been taught that Fucking and Killing are the two basic instincts – and Winning (or scoring as it is called) is the spur to them both. The thrill of winning and the thought of hanging my opponent always stimulates me. In the triumph and jubilation I am sometimes near to ejaculation. If the Hanging came first I doubt if I could guarantee another comparable stimulation for the Fucking. The players have to show success by holding up a full condom. Should I or any player fail to do this – we would be laughed and ridiculed and there would be no alternative but suicide.

Incidentally, a change in the order of the service could also affect the quality of the semen. At present it is collected after the Fuck which immediately follows The Game. It is at its best when most energised. If we donate after the Hanging – possibly from a second coming – the quality will be inferior. These are all factors to be borne in mind.

The Glossatores have billed the match this weekend as the most important for years. When I hang my former friend it will be the climax of my career. I will then retire. It will be my last game – as well as his. He helped me overcome a moment of weakness years ago. I have more than made up for it since. I am stronger than him now. We will conquer his team and I will ensure that all aspects of the proceedings are carried out thoroughly. Past friendship is no excuse for pity. Yet I know hanging him will stimulate me.

Please let the Powers not change the order of Procedures before this match.

Summon Up

DON'T WORRY ABOUT ALL THAT SHIT. I'll see it gets cleared up.'

'Very kind of you,' I say. 'I appreciate that.'

It looks as if the day might turn out better than expected. And, as so often, thanks in no small measure, to that young man.

Pleasant lad. Helpful when you need it. And that's the thing, isn't it? Not like the nurses fussing round just when you want to nod off. Or that bloody doctor. Never know when to expect him. Does his rounds a different time each day. At least you can hear his trolley coming. Needs someone to push it for him. Weedy little thing.

'Look what I've got for you today.'

How should I know what it is? This ometer, that ometer. Looks like something out the dashboard of a space ship. The graphs make you dizzy. And the language he talks is out this world. Catch him lifting a patient out of bed. Easing you into a chair. And as for turning the mattress!

But he, that young orderly, he reminds me of my batman.

The one I had all those years we were stationed ... Where was it? The name'll come to me. Bates. That was it. Bates. Wonder what his name is?

Most of them wear a name badge. Never got close enough to see his. They tell you anyway without asking. Always the first name. 'Call me Cynthia. I happen to be the matron here.' Not for much longer if I had my way.

They should have their names cut into their front teeth, a letter a tooth. Then the ones with short names wouldn't have to smile so much. Like Nurse Ann, beaming ear to ear, even if everyone's dying around her. And the ones with the long names – like that miserable cow Nurse Veronica – would have to crack their cheeks a bit more to identify themselves. I might put that in the suggestions box. They say it's anonymous. None of the usual comeback.

'Here, Bates, could you ... possibly ...?'

'You mean me?'

'Yes. You know I do.'

'My name's Henry.'

'Can't help that. If I'd wanted to call you by your first name I'd have looked on your medical records. You'll always be Bates to me.'

'Whatever you say.'

'And I shall always be Sir to you. Don't let's be forgetting that.'

'No. Sir.'

What a load of nonsense all these forms are! Style of

address. Underline as applicable. Mr, Mrs, Miss and the ubiquitous MS. What about Dr, Rev, Sir or Lord? Don't they count anymore? No hope for an ex-Colonel then, is there? Surprised they even ask for a family name.

And the address itself, the place of residence that is. Or subsidence. Who dreams up these names? Sunny Uplands Nursing Home. Why not Dump for Incurables?

Bates has been very loyal to me. That's how it should be, I know. But I've got to hand it to him. A lot of water under the bridge. Not everyone would have come back after the row we had. I rather went adrift once I left the services. Lot of cheap travel. Never back to places I'd been posted to. Sort of places I'd always said we should've bombed. Huh! Often wondered if I'd bump into him. It's good of him to have looked me up. I must have taken some finding.

He seems happy enough here, though there can't be much satisfaction. How he used to iron my uniform and shine my boots! What can you do with a gown and hospital slippers? Loyalty's the thing, isn't it? Asking no questions. And telling no lies.

Good God! How they make a fuss out of nothing! Total over-reaction. So, it's goodbye to Sunny Uplands. At least, it's not feet first.

I suppose it's all going to be put on my medical records. A red warning star. Incurable. A no hoper. A compulsive groper. Assign to female carers only.

Bates didn't mind. Never did. All in a day's work to him. No-one would've been any the wiser if that bitch Nurse Veronica hadn't burst in. All that shit about hospital etiquette. On and on, she went. She's the incontinent one. Obviously fancied him. Well, sorry to tell you. I know my man. You've got no chance of getting into his pants. Bang your head against the brick wall all you like.

I know I can rely on Bates. He'll check the records. Find out where I'm going to be posted next. He'll get a job there, too. Somehow. Wheedle his way in, whatever. I won't have to wait long.

Reverses in Time
Opening chapter of forthcoming novel
Push harder Mummy, I want to come out

I WAS BORN ON THE TWENTY-NINTH of February, Leap Year's Day, in the tenth year of my parents' otherwise childless marriage. My father was old enough to have been my grandfather. My mother was half his age; and joyless and dutiful. I doubt my birth brought them any rejuvenation. I myself had no childhood and was born middle-aged.

I was barely ten (in solar years, that is, or two-and-a-half in birthdays) when my father died. My mother failed to blossom and make the most of her loss. Within a year she was diagnosed as having a disease that would prematurely age her. It was almost poetically just. My parents had taken my childhood from me, and now one of them was dead and the other was going to age fifteen physical years for every solar one. I wouldn't, after all, have to wait for my mother to die before I could make up for lost time. Everything had changed, and I began to savour the reversal of rôles.

As a child I'd been taught the most exacting table manners. 'Sit up straight. Keep your mouth shut. Don't make a noise when you're eating. Don't talk with your mouth full. Hold your knife and fork properly. Put them down neatly between mouthfuls. Put them together when you've finished. Don't turn your fork over to spear peas. A knife is always necessary. You may eat cake with a fork. Be careful of your new clothes.'

The order 'Wear your bib' was eventually replaced by 'Don't drop anything on your tie.' In fact, a greater problem was dropping things on my trousers. At the age of eleven I spilled some ice-cream on the divide of my very first pair of long trousers. I splayed my legs, spat on a serviette and rubbed up and down vigorously on the stain. I'd expected Mother to say 'There's a good boy. You don't want to ruin your new trousers, do you?' Instead, she looked on in fascinated and speechless horror – as if I was doing something obscene. She never mentioned table manners again.

Other people have never failed to mention them. How exemplary! How polite! Foreign women in particular were later to think me a true English Gentleman.

And now the issue has arisen once more. For there is Mother, accelerated in the slowing-down process, doing all the things she told me not to do. She spills her food as her shaking hands don't quite coincide with her uncontrollably nodding head. Her false teeth clack on solid food, and her lips suck and slurp on liquids. She drops peas on the floor and crushes them into the carpet under her slippers.

Not only this. There's been a verbal regression. She's begun again to use those babyish simplifications of words that she once invented for my benefit. Creamy molk-

molk. Be-beff. Din-dins. Beautiful, isn't it? Boo-flins. Boo-flins din-dins.

I can still visualise her bulk hovering round my rickety baby form, thrusting a spoon into my mouth and making chicken-calling noises, suffixing every remark with a question tag, at which she smiles and nods – and expects me to do the same.

'Good. Isn't it? You like that. Don't you? Nice? Cluck! Cluck! Isn't it? More? Pop it in. You wanted that. Didn't you? Chew it first. Won't you? Don't swallow it straight-away. Will you?'

It reminds me now of those necessarily one-sided dialogues in the fellatio scenes of pornographic videos to which I've become so addicted. 'You like a big mouthful. Don't you? You do? Yeah? You wanna take it all in, eh? Suck that dick?'

Poor Mother! Her early discipline didn't have the long-term effects on me she desired.

Mirror, all those years ago, what was I like as a sperm? Am I to believe I was the fastest and most eager of the bunch, the one with the greatest sense of purpose? Surely, I'd be at the back of the queue, hardly aware of the starter's orders and just following in panic formation.

O my brothers, who perished in your millions! And left me alone. And my sisters, too! Not one left. Not the twin I longed to be re-united with.

What a relief for you all to be propelled from my father's flaccid old member, albeit not into the open, but into Mother's gravity-less time-tunnel. No wonder you all wanted to play around, uncurl, whip your tails and turn a somersault before getting down to the serious business of your first – and let's face it – only really important rat-race.

But I, I was serious from the start. I didn't want to play games. You pushed me ahead into the firing line. 'You go first,' you all chorused. 'You don't like playing games, do you?'

O my brothers, I can imagine you now joking around just like those rough boys my mother subsequently so warned me against, and to whom I'm now so addicted. How much I owe you, then as now. You did no harm. The only scrape you got into was a D&C. While I – a bird flying across the sun, or an innocent transparent shrimp swimming past a voracious sea-anemone – got inextricably engorged.

To be fair to myself I wasn't exactly bad at playing games. I just felt no enthusiasm for following the rules, or fitting in with the wishes of others. Of course, I liked the muscle-flexing and the camaraderie, and when forced to participate I spent most of the time ogling the other players. Nice little numbers, some of them, even at that age.

We had assembled full-clothed in the gym, the first PE lesson of the first week of secondary school, unfamiliar faces everywhere, dreading the arrival of a master who had the reputation of a tartar. After a ten-minute wait he strode in and told us to take off our shoes, socks and trousers, strip to the waist and line up in our underpants against the wall-bars in order of height.

I was observant and had always been good at sizing people up. I aligned between two boys, one just shorter and one just taller, so that I at least was in the correct position in relation to them. It proved more difficult for the less perceptive boys, and in the nervous rush a bad order was formed. The master sorted us out and then walked down the row making rhetorical comments about our height and the condition of our underpants.

'You're a big fellow, aren't you? Sprouted up early. Need filling out a bit, though. And you. Still wearing trousers. What's up? Disobedient? Deaf? Or not wearing pants? And as for you – where did you get those pants from? Your kid brother? Makes it stick out a bit, doesn't it?' And so on until the end of the row.

He then introduced himself. 'Name's Goodall. Hear that? Goodall. Now, you, what's the opposite of "good"?'

'Bad,' I replied.

'Good. And you,' pointing to another boy, 'What's the opposite of "all"?'

There was no reply. 'Come on. Don't any of you know? What? NONE of you?'

'None, sir,' we groaned.

'There, do you see. The opposite of my name is the same. Good-all. Bad-none. Ever come across an opposite that's the same before?'

He seemed highly amused. I realised this much-vaunted martinet was really a doddle. I had no difficulty in avoiding his lessons, with excuses about my mother's deteriorating health and having no father and being the only child, and so on. Eventually I didn't even bother with an excuse. I just arrived late – in time for the showers, which I loved.

How keenly I observed the boys! Their hair dampened from exercise, partly straightened by sweat on their foreheads and now totally flattened by the spray, the entangled forms enveloped in the steam, the emergent delineation of the musculature, the blossoming of the inverted triangles of pubic hair, the buttocks opening as the bar of soap was retrieved from the floor, the vigorous towelling down that caused a swaying of the willie. Is it roundhead or cavalier?

In time I found even these delights inadequate, as indeed I was later to find saunas and steam baths. I avoided games altogether – and most other lessons as well – and spent more time at home. I told Mother in her lucid moments that we had long free periods to study independently. I'd often come home early and say that I'd been studying at the local Public Library. Which was partly true. I never told her that the window seat at the Library gave a fine vista of the entrance to an adjacent public lavatory; a location which was more pleasing than any playing field and peopled with more interesting men – and devoted to what I now realised was my true sport.

'What did you do at school today?' Mother would say with a supreme effort of mental concentration and breath control.

'Maths. Approximation. Estimation. Conversion.'

'What does that involve?'

'You have to estimate the size of things and then convert the measurements.'

'I see,' and her head nodded uncontrollably. Of

course, she didn't see. Her mind had wandered even before she'd finished the sentence. But it must have been a great comfort to her that I'd continue a conversation even after she'd lost it.

'For instance,' I went on, 'if it's a good nine inches long then you multiply by 2.5 to get it in centimetres.'

I also skived off from that other communal school event – school meals. I took food from home, usually items that the home-help had prepared for Mother, but which had been left uneaten. I had to be very secretive when I fished the container out of my satchel as I'd be immediately surrounded by a group of boys. Some of them, even though they'd come straight from the school dining hall, would say 'Let's have a bit' or 'What's she given you today?' I kept them in tow, never fully satisfied but never going without – a principle I was to develop in later years. One lad often said, 'I wish I had a mother like yours.'

'Yes, I expect you do,' I said, greatly doubting it. I bribed him to do little jobs for me – including masturba-tion. But I wasn't really interested in my own age group. I liked the older men I saw from the Library window. They went wild over me. I'd return home from school wearing the casual clothes that had become de rigeur for our year, and then go to the public lavatory having changed into the school uniform – which was now far too small. But what advantage a collar undone, a tie askew, a rakish cap and a shirt tail hanging out! How they loved my growing-up and my unchanged cherubic looks! They gave me little tips – which I spent in the local sex shop on nude magazines, pornographic videos and bottles of poppers.

I was soon openly asking for tips. 'Can you help me?' I'd say in my most helpless voice. 'You couldn't make it a bit more, could you?' If necessary, I added 'I have an incapacitated mother at home.' If they questioned this I'd reel off a list of surgical appliances, medical routines and medicaments. Whether they believed me or not, they always thought me deserving of some recompense. Well, not pence. No coins, please. Notes in double figures. And many of them!

Of course, my truancy extended to subjects other than games. I made excuses, forged letters, claimed my mother was incapacitated, and everything fell on me, having no father, brothers or sisters and being an orphan, 'almost.' I did my work at the local Library, and read extensively far beyond the school syllabus. I overtook the clever pupils, the ones, who like the pace-setters in athletics, always burn out halfway through. The masters couldn't credit my progress. I made their work seem superfluous. I was summoned by my form master.

'You've been away a lot. I didn't realise quite how much.'

'It's my mother, sir. She's ninety-five.'

'Don't be silly. How can she be ninety-five when you're only fifteen?'

'It's the ageing process, sir. It's accelerated in her. For every one year we get older she ages fifteen. Next birthday, she's a hundred-and-ten.'

'I see.'

'It's not funny, sir.'

'I wasn't laughing.'

'A lot of people do, sir. That only makes it worse for me. It's a problem enough as it is.'

'I – I'm sorry,' he said contritely. 'I can imagine – I think – what you have to bear. Does the problem impede your ageing – I mean – your learning process?'

'I do my best, sir,' I said, sweetly. 'I spend a lot of time in the local lava – I mean Library.'

'That's good. Well-stocked, is it?'

'It's good enough for me, sir. I always hand the set-work in on time.'

'That's true – and very commendable.'

'Are any of the other masters cross with me, sir?' I asked in a plaintive voice.

'Not that I – well, not exactly but – let's put it this way. I don't think all the masters would be as understanding about these things as perhaps – er – I …'

'Oh, dear.'

'If there's any problem – if you want anything – you will come to me first, won't you? I wouldn't want you having to talk about your problems to everyone.'

'That's very kind of you, sir.'

'Here's my home telephone number. We must keep in touch,' he said, putting his hand on my shoulder. 'I hope circumstances improve. We all want to see a lot more of you.'

The master had been very good to me. I felt I had to repay him. That night in the public lavatory, as I sat idly and still fully-buckled in a cubicle, I wrote in indelible ink below the existing graffiti – 'For a really good time telephone …' and added the number he'd given me.

My school attendance did not improve. I spent more and more time studying in the Library. I was also able to save some of the money from my 'tips' to help Mother, for we weren't a particularly well-off family. Such private saving proved unnecessary. Mother's doctor intervened with even greater help.

The doctor had always treated me like a child (more so than Mother had before the onset of her illness). He warned me one day as I was showing him to the front door.

'Your Mummy – she's got a Dicky Ticker.' He patted himself on the chest to emphasise the point. 'I'm going to give her some quick-dissolving pills. She must pop them under her tongue. They work almost instantly. Under no circumstances must she get over-excited.'

'She's not likely to, is she? Housebound and confined to bed?'

'You'd be surprised the passions that can exist the less their outlet.'

I'll second that, I thought, and looked upon the doctor with new respect.

'She must also,' he continued, 'have access to all facilities. That's first and foremost a wheelchair.'

We had the door locks removed and replaced by ball catches. Mother was able to manoeuvre from room to room and open the doors by sticking out her legs or using her walking stick – another facility, metal, battle-ship grey, adjustable in length and with a rubber bung at the end.

'She must also,' added the doctor, 'have a home-help.'

There has been a whole succession of them. Few survive Mother's tantrums. She gets worked up if a speck of dust is missed, little realising the amount of dirt she creates herself. Anyway, she hates another woman in the house. (PROMISE Mummy – I'll never bring one home.) The very presence of a woman near her, even one on television, seems to rejuvenate her and slow down the ageing process.

The current home-help is Mrs Mansell, to whom Mother behaves like a tyrant, generating hatred and atmospherics. Happily, Mrs Mansell is meek, a bit deaf and forever ignorant of what she's supposed to have done. She never begins a conversation, merely answers questions and then only with question tags, invariably the wrong one. If I say 'What a lovely day,' she'll answer 'Hasn't it?' If I ask 'Have the groceries been delivered yet?' she'll reply 'Didn't they just?' You can say what you like and get the wrong response; but you can never rile her.

Last week I said 'What a lovely dress you've got on under your three-quarter length regulation overall.'

She replied, 'Didn't they?'

'Was it a present from one of your many gentlemen admirers?'

'Isn't it?'

Mother herself has very acute hearing. She hates anyone going into her bedroom. She listens intently whenever Mrs Mansell goes to do the cleaning. The bedroom is an inner sanctum, preserved unchanged since Father's time and decked out with beauty creams and scent bottles, pomanders, a cassolette and other vanities. Mother's favourite is an atomiser with a long lead ending in a small rubber oval, like a rugby ball. She positions the atomiser in the direction she wants it to spurt – usually behind her ear – and squeezes the ball with her elbow. She keeps it even nearer to the edge of the bed than the box containing the pills for her Dicky Ticker.

I like that expression – Dicky Ticker. At night when I'm in my own bedroom flicking through magazines and sniffing poppers and performing a clockwork (and to a lesser extent pendulum) action with my member I always think of the phrase and say it's Dicky Ticker Time. Under the onrush of the poppers to the head I feel I'm about to have a heart attack and listen aghast at the insistent pounding, which reverberates through the whole house – and which on most occasions turns out to be Mother calling for help, banging the rubber end of her walking stick into the pea-encrusted carpet.

And there she is – on the edge of the bed, the pill-box spilled over the floor – stretching out as far as she dares, her gnarled fingers gathering at the nearest pill. I pop it under her tongue and prop her up on the pillows. The bright redness of her face soon drains away, growing paler than her normal colour till she becomes the ghostly grey of cremated bone ash. The pill is having no effect. Her breathing is becoming slower and more laboured. I cannot find her pulse.

I panic, run to my room, grab the bottle of poppers and thrust it under her nose, flattening each nostril in turn. She flushes bright red, bugs out her eyes and begins breathing heavily. I tuck her up and pick up the bedside phone to call the doctor. She cuts me off, shakes her head and stretches out for the bottle. I put it down among her scent bottles. She smiles her gratitude.

She has little time for the doctor now, but has come to look on me as her special saviour. The bottle of poppers has been given pride of place, next to the atomiser. I must say she gets through it at a remarkable pace. I feel less furtive now in my ever more frequent visits to the sex shop. Buying things there for one's mother certainly cuts down on any feelings of guilt!

More stories by John Dixon:

THE CARRIER BAG AND OTHER STORIES

Ten stories. Varied topics, forms and lengths.

'The Carrier Bag' is a Bridport prize-winning story, of which Margaret Drabble said 'A tale for our time, which satirically contrasts a wine bar squash-playing set with a representative member of the underclass. A fine use of dialogue here, from a writer who has his ear to the ground.'

In 'Across the Corridor – and Down a Bit' a knowing holiday diarist unfailingly gets it wrong. In 'Something Was Up', a fictional memoir, a perplexed grown-up reflects on the year his mother had a hysterectomy at the same time as his elder sister came of age. 'Little Gems' is a mother's monologue on her three daughters. 'The Untoward Invention' is a political satire telling how an invention of potential use in waste disposal is seconded by the War Ministry. In 'Coping' a patient reacts to a marriage guidance counsellor's trite recommendations. 'The Heights' concerns a Christmas postman who is given a round no one else wants. 'Well our feeble frame...' tells of the Damascus Road incidents of a middle-aged woman on holiday in Jordan. 'Consequences' asks if apparent results are so easily traceable to assumed causes. 'Inconsequences' is the erratic diary confessional of an employee losing control.

Paradise Press: ISBN 978-1-904585-40-4